THAAMBA

STOP. DO NOT ENTER

Jaidev

INDIA • SINGAPORE • MALAYSIA

Copyright © Jaidev 2022
All Rights Reserved.

ISBN 979-8-88749-310-7

This book has been published with all efforts taken to make the material error-free after the consent of the author. However, the author and the publisher do not assume and hereby disclaim any liability to any party for any loss, damage, or disruption caused by errors or omissions, whether such errors or omissions result from negligence, accident, or any other cause.

While every effort has been made to avoid any mistake or omission, this publication is being sold on the condition and understanding that neither the author nor the publishers or printers would be liable in any manner to any person by reason of any mistake or omission in this publication or for any action taken or omitted to be taken or advice rendered or accepted on the basis of this work. For any defect in printing or binding the publishers will be liable only to replace the defective copy by another copy of this work then available.

Dedication

This book is dedicated to the memory of my sister-in-law, late Mrs Guntur Chinnammai, without whose active participation it would not have been possible for me to travel the length and breadth of Rayalaseema and to have gained a wealth of information about the region, she was and will always be remembered by us, as a very warm and lovable person whom I, my wife Santhi and my daughter Pavithra will miss deeply.

Disclaimer

This book is purely a work of fiction, all names of all persons mentioned in this book is purely fictitious and based on the author's imagination. The descriptions of events, places, buildings, houses, mansions, people either living or dead and their occupations described herein is fictitious. This book is not based on any historical fact or occurrence, any similarity or resemblance in the names of people either living or dead, events and places mentioned in this book is purely coincidental and unintentional.

Jaidev

(The Author)

The Flag of the Rayas

"The Biggest Suspense in life is that you do not know who is praying for you and who is playing with you"

"Your ability to unravel this suspense in your life will decide whether you are going uphill or downhill"

Contents

Acknowledgement

My earlier book "Handi Biryani & A Wedding Suit" was well received by the readers. "Thaamba" my second book is a thriller, which is based on a zamindar and his family some time in the 18th century, the book describes various aspects of zamindari life, as it was, based on fragmented bits of information collected and collated from a host of records ie not from a single well documented record, intertwined with fiction. There are aspects which deal with the nature of life in general, pilgrimages, traditions & customs, hunting, lesser known facts about slavery, concubinage, wars and the pernicious effect of zamindars woven into an occult fabric. I have made a concerted attempt to write about an age about which very little is known, a period in history which was torn by tremendous strife, a plethora of emotions, sleaze, coquetry, immoral relationships and an overriding greed for wealth and power which finally leads to the downfall and the damnation of the zamindar.

I would like to take this opportunity to thank my wife Mrs. Santhi G Jaidev and my daughter Ms. Pavithra P Jaidev for their, love, unstinting support and constant encouragement.

I would like to take this opportunity to thank my sister-in-law, Mrs G.Chinnammai and her son

Mr Sivarama Krishna Deepak for taking me and my family around very many places in Rayalaseema region of the state of Andhra Pradesh in India and to acquaint me with the topographical features, ancient temples, local customs, food habits, folklore, cultural and social aspects concerning the people of this region.

(All paintings with the water mark Jaidev Arts depicted in this book are proprietary paintings of the author.) I would like to thank one and all in Notion Press, my publishers for their goodwill, cooperation and for giving shape to this book.

All copy rights rest with the author, no part of this publication may be reproduced, stored in a retrieval system or transmitted in any form or by any means electronic, mechanical, recording or otherwise for any purpose without the prior, written permission of the author.

Jaidev S Gurudev

RTC House, Arakkonam

Tamilnadu, India 2021/22

Author's Note

Many years ago as a young employee, I was busy sketching a small shark in one corner of my diary, my colleague who was watching me said "do you feel like someone is biting you", I said "how did you guess that", he said "I thought that you drew a shark because in your subconscious mind someone is biting you, which causes you pain". Fiction writing is like the shark I drew. On the face of it there was no meaning that can be ascribed to it, but on looking a little deeper, the drawing was the conscious manifestation of the pain caused to me by a senior employee, which was rooted in my subconscious mind. In this book I have described the remnants of victims as mere skull and bones with hair, teeth and with a sallow clothing of skin. This description which appears like fiction has very deep roots in my subconscious mind, in the sense that when I wrote these lines I was not actively thinking about anyone in particular, but was actually describing a person whom I knew and who in life gave the impression of someone whose life sustaining vigour and vitality had been sucked out leaving behind a body that appeared to be long since dead. Remember my dear readers that:

"Much of conscious fiction is rooted in subconscious
facts, the repository of such facts is
the subconscious mind"

– Jaidev

Painting: The Cross Roads

(All paintings with the water mark Jaidev Arts are proprietary paintings of the author)

"It is a mistake to fancy that horror is associated inextricably with darkness, silence and solitude"

– H. P. Lovecraft

Prologue

We returned from Madanapalli where we had gone to do some shopping and to have lunch. By around 5 pm in the afternoon we slowly wound our way over the vast muddy, boulder, stone and cobble strewn countryside to the entrance of a zamindari property at Mahadevpalli. Right at the entrance was a massive black granite stone arch, the height of the arch at its highest point must have been about twenty five feet above the ground. On either side of this stone arch, supporting it were massive stone pillars which must have measured at least about eighteen feet in height, the stone pillars were completely overrun by a creeper or a vine with long tendrils, very similar to the common money plant except that the leaves were much bigger and the tendrils were very much longer and robust. The creeper added an element of colour, greenery and its flowers added beauty to an otherwise dull and drab countryside, the fragrance exuded by the flowers was divine. I decided that on the way out, I would definitely take a few cuttings of this exquisite plant. The arch was covered up to a certain extent but a major portion of the arch especially the portion above the gate was not covered by the creeper. Perched on these stone pillars was a pair of grotesque stone gargoyles with wings. The stone pillars supported two very ancient and very heavy wrought iron gates which were also overrun by the same creeper, the height of each gate was about fifteen feet. Extending on either side of the gate was a creeper covered wall with a parallel row of stunted trees with very stout trunks, the height of this stone wall was around fifteen feet.

The iron gates of this zamindari estate were wide open, as if it did not matter who entered. Well ahead of the gate on one side was a massive stone edict embedded in the ground, the above ground portion of the stone edict had a height of about five feet and a width of around three or four feet. Carved on this edict was the palm of a human hand with the fingers held together with red kumkum or vermillion (a red powder which is applied by Indians on their forehead to ward off evil) powder smeared on it, probably the work of a village vagabond, with the words **"Thaamba"** inscribed below the palm. Because I was acquainted with a number of Indian languages I was able to make out that the word, written in Marathi (Marathi is written using Devanagari alphabets which are slightly different from Hindi alphabets) meant **STOP**. I rolled down the glass windows of the vehicle and carefully read what was inscribed below the word "Thaamba" in Telugu. There was no necessity for me to get down to read what was inscribed on the stone edict because it was close enough for me to reach out and touch it.

It was a hot afternoon and the air conditioning inside our car was running at maximum capacity to ensure that everyone inside the car was comfortable which included the three of us, the driver Suresh and Bilal, a young medical assistant who was sent by my cousin Ramesh to show us around the country side. As we entered the estate a monitor lizard measuring approximately three to five feet in length from the head to the tip of the tail crossed our path. The driver was driving very slowly and he was able to prevent our vehicle from running over the lizard. We progressed a little further on the road when in the rays of the setting Sun we could see the massive outline of the mansion built over 300 years ago by the Zamindar Shankar Dev Rao. The mansion must have been built over at least three acres of land and surrounding it was open land with dry grass, shrubs dotted with mango, palm trees and very stout but stunted trees with leaves and flowers similar to the leaves on the vines, the girth of the trees indicated that they must have been hundreds of years old. All of this grew on an area roughly measuring at least a few hundred acres. At that moment I distinctly heard the high pitched cry of a child and I looked around to see whether anyone was around with a child but there was no one. Nothing grew on this open space in front of the house except for small stunted trees from which at close quarters I noticed the vines emerged, many more monitor lizards scurried past our vehicle, it was quite evident that this house did not have a visitor for a very very long time, the lizards were used to living there without any kind of hindrance or threat from anyone.

I noticed that Bilal, inspite of the airconditioning, was looking very sick and I also noticed that he was sweating profusely. By this time we were in front of the mansion, it was truly a majestic building with high colonnades of Corinthian pillars, a beautiful fountain in front and a very imposing frontage. The main door which was made of very old wood, probably teak wood was wide open. The walls of this massive mansion were covered by the same beautiful creeper or vine that covered the gates and the perimeter walls. We were about half a kilometre from the entrance when I decided that we should walk the rest of the way to the open doorway of the mansion at the end of approximately four flights of stairs. I told the driver to stop the vehicle. I rolled down my window, the fragrance in the air was not just divine, it was intoxicating and enticing. I once again heard a child crying followed by someone calling out. I was certain the mansion was inhabited, I thought some poor beggar and his family was staying in it and it was their child that I heard crying.

At this point our escort Bilal with great difficulty told me "Sahab, please turn back, it will be dark soon." I said "yes, we will just look around as long as there is sunlight, and then we will get back." Bilal said "Sahab, please in the name of Allah, let us leave this place without any delay." I was getting irritated so I snapped at Bilal "what is wrong with you." Bilal said "this place reeks of evil." I looked at Bilal and choosing my words carefully I asked him "what do you know about this place or about this house which you are not telling me." Bilal said "Sahab, all I know is that there are no villages within a vicinity of ten kilometers from this place, the villagers in this place as you know are extremely poor and live in small shacks made of stone and slate, they could have pulled down this building and used the stone and the teak wood to construct their houses but they did not do that. Infact they do not bring their cattle or goats to graze within five kilometres of this place." I said "Bilal, your story is interesting but it may be that the poor, uneducated villagers are superstitious and there is really no cause for concern." Bilal said "no" with finality and then he continued "sahab, did you read the inscription on the stone tablet at the entrance", I said I read "Thaamba" was inscribed on the tablet which means "stop" in Marathi. Bilal said "sahab, you obviously did not get the full meaning of what else was written on that tablet." The meaning of the other words on that edict written in Telugu means "do not enter", the combined meaning is "stop, do not enter." I said "oh, why not, what is the problem, who is going to stop me."

Bilal said "no one will stop you, all I know is that whatever is in there feeds on warm blooded animals." My wife who was patiently hearing this conversation intruded to say "let us go back", then she asked Bilal "do you know anyone who knows the history of this place?" Bilal said "yes, my great grandfather who stays in Gudupalli and is over 100 years old, may be in a position to answer some of your questions, because despite his age he is fit as a fiddle and his mind is razor sharp."

We decided to go back. On the way out I wanted to take a few cuttings of the creeper, but my wife dissuaded me from doing so on the the grounds that we would come back in broad daylight and collect any number of cuttings. While driving out of the main gate in the dim evening light before it became totally dark, I noticed a dozen vultures perched on the stone arch over the gate which was free of creepers, it was distinctly ominous.

The sun had set, except for the light cast on the road by our vehicle's head lights, there was pitch darkness all around us and a peculiar silence had descended which was akin to the "silence of the graveyard". We arrived at my cousin's place in Tondavada, in pindrop silence, all that we did on the way back was to drink the cold lassi that my relative had sent along in a flask along with disposable paper cups.

My dear friends, for those who want to know why the mansion evoked such fear, read on, to discover that whatever inhabited the mansion, had the ability to draw, to sense, to plan, to mimic, to ambush and for all practical purposes it was sinister and dangerous, it consumed not out of hunger but out of a desire to devour it's victims.

"Normal is an illusion. What is normal for the Spider is chaos for the fly"

– Charles Addams

Chapter 1

A Celestial Appearance

About 1000 years before the birth of Jesus Christ, a comet was seen over much of Rayalseema and the neighbouring areas of Kolar. A comet was looked upon as an omen which shed particles from a dusty tail with a head or a nucleus consisting of rock, ice and gas. As the earth passed through the tail of a comet, rocky debris collided with the atmosphere, creating a meteor shower. On this occasion, billions of shards of rock, some of them as large as a football field weighing several tonnes, which formed a part of the meteor shower, fell on the earth mainly in Rayalseema and its adjoining areas going upto Kolar. All the meteors in a meteor shower appeard to come from a single point in the sky called the radiant point or simply the radiant. Some meteors which are very large are called fireballs, these fireballs are brighter, larger and longer lasting than smaller earth grazers.

Apart from meteors, meteoroids which are massive lumps of rock and iron which orbit the sun also fell on that night. These meteoroids entered the earth's mesosphere and in the process heated up because of the tremendous friction caused by the hurtling pieces of rock as they sliced through the earth's atmosphere at a velocity ranging from 25,000 mph to 72,000 mph. As a result of this friction, the outer surface of the meteoroid caught fire and it glowed like a streak of light going past the night sky which made people refer to them as shooting stars or falling stars. A lot of superstitious people felt that making a wish at the very moment they saw the shooting or the falling star going past would be fulfilled. Unlike comets which people feared, falling stars were harbingers of good fortune.

The meteors and the meteoroids broke up into smaller fragments due to the heat caused by friction, on entering the earth's atmosphere. Some portion was completely burnt to ashes and the remaining rocky debris crashed on the hills to the south of the rocky and boulder strewn plains of Rayalaseema, setting ablaze a vast section of the forested area. Apart from the cauldron of raging fire, the meteors also created very deep fissures and craters due to the force of the impact. The force of the impact at the point of contact, as a giant meteor fell on the earth, travelling at a very great velocity, resulted in the temperature shooting up to 2000 degrees centigrade which led to the instantaneous crystallization of aromatic hydrocarbons of plant origin resulting in the formation of diamonds. At lower temperatures of about 1300 degrees centigrade saturated hydrocarbons of the same plant origin crystallized to form diamonds.

Over a period of time when water from underground aquifers found a fault or a fissure in the earth's crust, the water flowed to the surface bringing diamonds with it. With the flow of water overground, streams and rivulets carried the diamonds and deposited it on their banks, estuaries and further down on the banks of rivers and riverine islands. In this way the diamonds found their way to places as far away as Guntur. The availibiity of diamonds was responsible for the establishment of the Guntur & Golkonda Diamond Mining Company by the Nizam of Hyderabad, with the focus on mining diamonds, from the area within the Golconda fortress in Hyderabad and from Guntur. The diamonds were collected initially from 32 smaller locations spread in and around the two locations mentioned above and along the banks of the Krishna River. These flawless blue and pink diamonds made the Nizam the richest man in the world at a particular point of time in history. The diamonds were also used by the Nizam in the form of jewellery made by Hyderabad's skilled jewellers to be worn by over 3000 women in his harem i.e the wives or concubines of a polygamous man, usually someone belonging to the royalty, a Mughal, a Sultan or a Maharaja. The remaining flawless diamonds in large numbers found their way into the market place where merchants displayed them in small baskets and sold individual pieces to buyers, in those days, sitting on the ground outside the Charminar, just as semi precious stones, beads, amulets and finger rings are sold in the very same place today.

Apart from diamonds the meteors had a large amount of semi precious stones which was strewn across the forests to the south and a smaller percentage was strewn across the stony and rocky plains of Rayalaseema.

At this juncture it is important for me to inform the reader that sometime between 2006 and 2007, the South African diamond mining company "De Beers" spent a lot of time carefully mapping the areas in Rayalaseema. According to their study by skilled geologists who had considerable experience in prospecting for diamonds and other precious/semi precious stones, there was a sufficient quantity available in this place and for this purpose they were willing to spend on setting up an extraction unit. However due to bureaucratic red tapism and strong opposition from the ruling government at that time, the project was shelved.

In addition to semi precious stones the meteors brought clusters of free floating inert microorganisms which attached themselves to the meteorites and on entering the earth's atmosphere and finding ambient conditions and a substrate, got reactivated. Some of these microorganisms in the form of retro viruses caused genetic mutations in plants and animals. Some mutations were transmitted from generation to generation and were useful to the plant or the animal. In other cases, the mutations led to diseases which weakened the plant or the animal and in some cases resulted in the death of that plant or animal, at times the whole species was wiped out.

At the other end of the spectrum some viral DNA which came with the meteors used its own genes to copy itself, inserting those copies elsewhere in the plant or animal host's genomes. These genomes expressed themselves in different parts of the body, in the form of symbiotic relationships. A symbiotic retrovirus enabled the evolution of placenta over many generations in female animals which was necessary, for the foetus to mature inside the mother's uterus and allowed the entry of oxygen and nutrients, while removing waste and keeping the blood supplies for both purposes separate.

As against the integration of the genomes into the host over a considerable period of time there were other changes which occurred in a very short span of time and under extreme conditions called spontaneous mutations. These mutations brought about drastic changes in the behaviour, food habits of plants and animals and many of these mutations were passed on from generation to generation. One such mutation occurred in a plant which started to grow like a sea anemone from a normal height, to a height in excess of 20 feet, firmly rooted to the ground with branches like tentacles extending upto 20-25 feet. The giant plant, due to the effect of mutation and to survive in nitrogen deficient soils became carnivorous. There were other plants and animals whose characteristics had changed drastically but they managed to camouflage the changes in a manner that they appeared harmless.

In due course of time, in the 10thcentury AD, a very large number of people from Rayalaseema and Kolar, fearing an invasion by an enemy, moved further into the forested area to the south and trekked for months together, going through leech infested areas, plagued by malaria causing mosquitoes, attacked by swarms of vampire bats, ambushed by giant man eating pythons, mauled and eaten by carnivorous fish and animals, weakened by blood sucking insect parasites and by incessant rains, along with which came another host of diseases. They crossed high mountain ranges, raging streams and water falls, went through very deep almost impenetrable jungles and caves from one end, hacking their way through the undergrowth. There were times when the jungle seemed to be a tangle of vines, stalks and leaves. Finally as they saw a vast opening while reaching the jungle's edge with only a few vines blocking the way. Someone struck down a thick vine slicing it in two and all of a sudden there was the high pitched sound of someone wailing, similar to the sound of a lot of women weeping in unison in the darkness. Lit dimly by star light, it was as if the whole jungle had come alive, a clearing appeared as if something that was obstructing the view had moved aside and then a number of snake like appendages wrapped around the body of the unfortunate victims, knocking the victims off their feet. Then, whatever had grabbed them, dragged the victims screaming in terror, through the jungle to something gigantic which may have been of animal or plant origin and thrust the victims, bodily, into an opening at the top. Thereafter each victim be it a man, a woman or a child disappeared from sight one by one. The giant carnivore had eaten and would be ready after a month or so, to eat once again after digesting the victims and excreting the waste through very thick roots or veins which went deep into the ground. From thousands who initially undertook the harrowing journey through this forested area, only a small number survived.

"May be all the schemes of the devil were nothing compared to what man could think up".

– Joe Hill

Chapter 2

Surya Samrajyam

Those who survived the ordeal through the jungle were those who had survived because they were the fittest among both men and women. The jungle had ensured that only those who could make it through all the hardships survived. These men and women banded together, intermarried and created the Surya Samrajyam or the Kingdom of the Sun God, governed by rules put in place by the council of elders. They depended initially on the forest to provide them with food items. Then they started to make implements and with the implements, they used domesticated animals, which they had brought along with them through the forest, such as bulls to plough the land, cows for milk, goats for their milk and mutton, sheep for their wool and mutton, chicken and ducks as food. They used the seeds that they had brought along to grow small quantities of rice, wheat, maize, millets and pulses in a small area, the acreage grew in time.

All this took a long long time and was by no means an easy task. In the meantime, the inhabitants had discovered that deep in the jungle there were places where blue and pink diamonds along with semi precious stones were deposited by mountain streams on their banks. The discovery of diamonds and semi precious stones made the inhabitants very wealthy.

Simultaneous to this discovery, their priests and druids had discovered that drinking a decoction made from the leaves of the mulberry bush, parasitized by a peculiar worm which made the plant the repository of a virus that was responsible for the manipulation of human genes, to create superior human beings, with resistance to a number of diseases and with physical traits such as a uniform nut brown skin colour, jet black hair, a good physique with a lot of stamina, strong dentures, very sharp eyesight and an acute sense of hearing. Drinking the viral decoction also ensured that full grown males and females were fairly tall. The females were endowed with firm breasts and a grown up in the age group 16 to 17 belonging to both sexes had fully developed genetalia, without any deformity which ensured that when they indulged in sex for procreation, their progeny had all that was best and brightest in them. Any recessive traits that the parents may have had were suppressed in the progeny. In other words they were making their children according to a set design, not just begetting them, that would have introduced an element of non-design and random selection. Some people may argue that begetting i.e non-design is critical to human dignity and human rights, because what you beget is a product of your free decision, leaving human evolution to the processes of natural selection. Whereas what you make, as in this case, was the product of using a virus to enhance certain traits and qualities while suppressing others, which the council of elders in the kingdom of the Sun God considered base, recessive and undesirable.

With the passage of time, like all communities, the inhabitants of the Kingdom came to believe, based on their own texts written by their elders over the centuries, that they were the direct progeny of the Sun God and from then on they called themselves the Suryavanshis ie decendants of the Sun God and believed that they belonged to the family of the Sun God ie Suryavansham and that their kingdom was Surya Samrajyam or the Kingdom of the Sun. In due course of time they developed their own rituals and came to accept the giant sea anemone like tree with sharp spines as their living God called Prachanda Deva. The inhabitants of the kingdom firmly believed that Prachanda Deva was the living incarnation or the living embodiment of the Sun God and for their living God they built a massive stone temple shaped like a Roman collesium in the midst of which the living God grew.

The council of elders had framed very stong rules with regard to certain matters and any infringement or attempt to disregard the rules which was passed on to the inhabitants of the kingdom by word of mouth, was punishable with death. The council of elders did not have any discretionary powers to spare one person while punishing another for the same offence nor did they have powers to dilute the punishment for any reason whatsoever. Divorce was unheard of and not permitted, adultery was not permitted and causing grievous injury to anyone and indulging in any kind of bestiality by engaging in irregular or perverse sex was strictly forbidden. These offences were punishable with death. Since the inhabitants were very wealthy they were allowed to have two wives and maintain two families. Despite a positive male to female ratio of one male to every two females there was a shortage of females and this shortage was made up by allowing small groups of young men with a middle aged mentor to leave the kingdom, after negotiating the impenetrable wall of carnivores, through a hidden, underground tunnel the location of which was known only to three seniormost members of the council of elders. The members of the group would be blindfolded and taken through the tunnel by a member, who knew about its exact location, to a far off point well within the jungle, where the blindfold was taken off and each member of the group armed with a bow, poisoned arrows, a knife and a wooden jar holding water, was allowed to go from their kingdom further into the dense jungle and then to undertake the arduous task of crossing the jungle. They took several months to cross the forests, high mountain ranges and other obstacles similar to that which was faced by those who came through the jungle and established the kingdom deep within the jungle. Nothing much had changed even after a considerable period of time, but, because these men were the product of genetic manipulation, it gave them a lot more strength and the stamina to endure hardships, they were able to reach the outside world without any fatalities.

Once they reached the world outside, the group became busy in establishing itself as a small group of well established diamond merchants. Slowly they disposed off the diamonds in their possession in exchange for gold jewellery and gold currency, they also let it be known that they were on the lookout for beautiful, well built, homely girls to marry and for this purpose many prospective parents and their young daughters in the age group, between 16 to 18, thronged their residence. After all the members of the group got married and after a couple of months the group on the pretext of undertaking a pilgrimage (after settling all outstanding issues including monetary issues pertaining to the bridegroom's parents and younger siblings if any), undertook the arduous task of returning through the jungle back to the kingdom of the Sun God where the newly married women were given the viral decoction prepared by the druids to prepare them for procreation (husbands engaged in sex with the pupose of inseminating their wives only after their wives drank the viral decoction, earlier to that the couples took pains to ensure that sex did not lead to insemination and pregnancy). This infusion of fresh females into the population pushed up the percentage of females considerably over a period of thirty years, the sex ratio had risen, for every one male there were three females and even if one individual married two females the remaining men still had an able bodied women to marry, the population of the kingdom grew manifold. The inclusion of females from outside also prevented, inbreeding depression.

As mentioned in the earlier part of this narrative the council of elders framed certain rules which could not be broken for fear of being punished with death. Unfortunately once in a while there were people who broke the rules and on the appointed day i.e on a full moon night the entire inhabitants of the kingdom assembled in the colosseum like open air temple, the condemned prisoner was doused in the blood of an animal and given an alcoholic drink which numbed the senses, then the prisoner was prodded with long sticks to enter the enclosure of the living God whom the inhabitants called "Prachanda Deva" which means someone gigantic and frightening. The serpent like appendages of the living God sensed blood and a warm living body, they came alive and suddenly wrapped themselves around the prisoner, dragging him and dropping him into an opening at the top of the giant sea anemone like plant or animal, the opening closed and the prisoner was digested by powerful fluids within the plant/animal. Thereafter the residents of the kingdom returned to their houses, bathed and slept on an empty stomach, no sex was permitted on that night, this was done as a mark of respect to the dead man. Womenfolk were considered as inferior to the menfolk and those women who indulged in any activity which resulted in breaking the rules set out by the council or were instrumental in inducing a man to break the rules, were unceremoniously shunted out of the kingdom into the forest to fend for themselves, some of them survived for a few months in the jungle, others perished sooner.

In the following years as the population grew there was a fresh need to look at the security of the kingdom and for this purpose three more concentric rings infested with carnivores was added. This prevented anyone from trying to enter the kingdom. Those who tried were repulsed by the carnivores, those who persisted paid the price with their life. This living fortress also ensured that the wealth of the kingdom remained within the kingdom and also ensured that the source of the diamonds and the semi precious stones remained a closely guarded secret. Only those who were permitted by the council of elders to leave the kingdom along with a mentor for the world outside were taken out of the kingdom through the secret tunnel as mentioned earlier.

At this juncture it is imperative that, I pause my narrative to inform the reader about a few facts pertaining to man eating plants. In the kingdom of the Sun the inhabitants accepted "Prachanda Deva" as the living version of the Surya or the Sun God in the 10th century AD ie a 1000 years after the birth of Christ and the establishment of the Christian calendar.

It is very interesting to note that a man eating plant, the subject of folklore and legend concerning the kingdom of the Sun God has found mention in a non-fiction book published in 1887 called "Sea And Land" by James W. Buel in which the author describes the Yateveo as a plant native to Africa and Central America, so named because it produced a hissing sound similar to the Spanish word "Ya-te-veo" which means "Now I See You". This giant carnivorous tree had poisonous spines resembling many huge serpents which pierced and seized the victim and sqeezed the blood out of the victim, the "dry carcass was thrown out and the trap set again".

Chase Osborn who became Governor of Michigan, in his book "Land of the Man Eating Tree" claimed that the tribes and missionaries on Madagascar knew about the hideous tree and repeated the account given by Karl Liche a German explorer, his companion Hendrick and members of the Mkodo tribe, who described an encounter with an atrocious cannibal tree with a base like a pineapple which had long leaves and tendrils. When a native woman went too close, the tree which appeared to be inert and lifeless, came to life and the tendrils with the fury of starved serpents grabbed her, the leaves closed in, the tendrils like green serpents wrapped around her with the savage tenacity of an anaconda and while the air was rent with her awful screams she was drawn into the plant, a short while later only a mix of plant fluid and her blood swept down the trunk.

In another instance William Thomas Stead, editor of the Review of Reviews, published an article in October 1891 about Mr Dunstan a well known naturalist from New Orleans who had returned from Central America where he had spent two years studying the flora and the fauna, related an incident that took place near one of the swamps that surrounded the great lakes of Nicaragua. According to him, he was hunting for botanical and entomological specimens when he heard his dog cry out, when he went closer to the spot where his dog was yelping in pain, he found his dog ensnared in a perfect network of what looked like rope like tentacles. With great difficulty he retrieved his dog but in the process patches of the dogs skin and flesh was torn away by infinitesimal mouths or little suckers on each tentacle. The locals called it the "Devil's snare". In Phil Robinsons book "Under the Punkah Tree" written in 1881, the author's uncle found a tree with "great waxen flowers" and "great honey drops" of fruits, with leaves that open and close like tiny hands. A little boy ran into a thicket of the tree's leaves, there was a stifled, strangling scream and except for the agitation in the leaves where they closed in on the boy, all signs of life had been obliterated.

During a voyage to the South Pacific led by the explorer Captain Arkwright in 1581, a man eating flower was described in the ship's log book.The captain described a very large flower with bright petals that released a sleep inducing toxin, which made the victim go to sleep on its petals. Once the victim was fast asleep the flower closed in and digested the victim alive, there was no telltale signs of any violence.

The great Biologist Charles Darwin was fascinated by these plants and spent fifteen years of his life studying them, Darwin initially called them "insectivores" but in later years scientists decided that the plants ate enough animals to be classified as "carnivores".

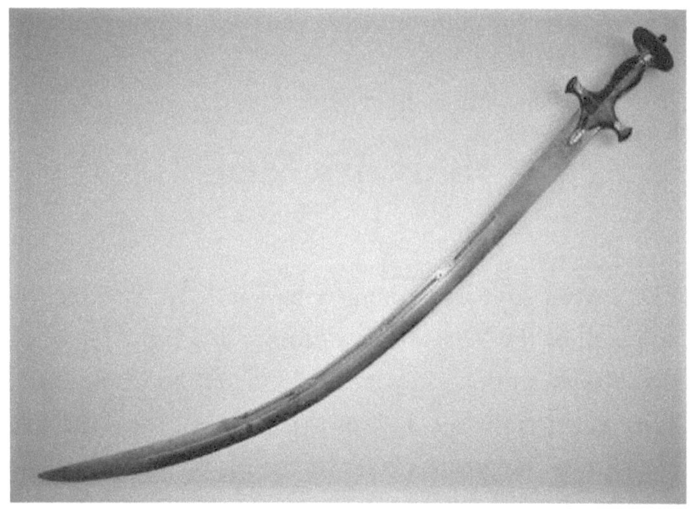

Maratha Sword

Chapter 3

Shivaji's Men

The Nayak Dynasty emerged in South India after the downfall of the Vijayanagara Empire in 1565 AD, when the Nayak military governors declared independence. They ruled from the 16th to the 18th century, Tirumala Nayak was the greatest ruler of the Nayak Dynasty. The Nayak rulers were noted for their administrative reforms, artistic and cultural achievements and the creation of a unique style of temple architecture.They also renovated temples sacked by the Delhi Sultans. The Tanjavur School of painting, a famous South Indian school of painting, emerged under the Nayaks.

There are many distinguishing features of Nayak temple architecture as pioneered by the Balija Nayak rulers of Madurai and Tanjavur i.e who were rulers of Telugu origin. Among the main characterstics of these temples were long corridors, carved hundred pillared and thousand pillared mandapas (outdoor temple halls or porches) and multi storied gopurams (towers adorning the entrance of a temple), richly decorated with brightly painted stone statues of animals, Gods and demons. Arguably the greatest example of the Nayak style of architecture is the Meenakshi Amman temple in Madurai which was built between 1623 and 1655 AD. The temple has 10 ornate gopurams, a hall with 985 pillars, each of which is a sculpture in the Dravidian style.

The Nayak ruler Chokkanatha placed his younger brother on the throne of Tanjavur, but within a year he overthrew his allegiance to the Nayak which forced the Nayak ruler to recognise the independence of Tanjavur until Venkoji (a half brother of the Maratha King Shivaji) became the first Raja of Tanjavur from the Bhosale dynasty and he is credited with the composition of the "Dvipada Ramayana in Telugu". The Tanjavur Maratha Rajas favoured Sanskrit and Telugu in their writing. Venkoji's descendants ruled Tanjavur until the death of the last descendant Shivaji-1 who reigned from 1832 to 1855. Shivaji-1 had no heir, under the circumstances the Queen adopted her nephew so that he could be coronated as the new ruler of Tanjavur. But the British authorities during the British Raj in India did not accept the proposal to place the nephew on the throne, instead they annexed Tanjavur under the provisions of the Doctrine of Lapse.

Apart from the developments in Madurai and Tanjavur the other great development that took place (which a lot of people in India are unaware of) was, when the city of Madras or Madraspatnam as it was known then, was just 38 years old in 1677 AD, it faced one of the greatest challenges to its survival, an invasion by Chatrapati Shivaji. Prior to this, Shivaji had on two occasions in 1664 AD and again in 1670 AD plundered Surat but had not been able to penetrate the defences of the English ie the defences of British East India Company. In 1665

Sir William Langhorne, the Governor of Madras was succeeded by Stereynsham Master as Governor of Fort St George, who had earlier on commanded the English forces in Surat and almost the first issue he had to deal with was the impending invasion of Chatrapati Shivaji. Shivaji's forces captured Vellore and Gingee (Jinji ruled by the Senji rulers of Tamil Nadu) and camped on the outskirts of Madras. The English forces in Fort St.George were rattled and decided to strengthen the defences of the city. But nothing happened. Shivaji's forces moved on and after conquering Gingee and Vellore, his forces reappeared in 1678 near Kanchipuram. Despite Shivaji's desire to conquer the fort at Poonamalle and then lay waste to Sadraspatnam, Madraspatnam and Pulicat, he abruptly decided to turn back. However there is an unconfirmed report that Shivaji a master at disguise did come to Madras and worshipped at the temple of Kaliambal on Tambu Shetty street, it was a well known fact that the great Maratha warrior was a worshipper of Goddess Bhavani. A portrait of Shivaji on horseback still hangs on the walls of the ancient temple, the date of Shivaji's visit on this portrait is October 16th, 1677. Why Shivaji turned back is an enigma, had he not turned back, Madras would have been inhabited by Marathi manoos ie people of Marathi origin.

One of the sainanis or soldiers in the army of Chatrapati Shivaji which came to the south was a young man called Vittal Dev Rao who settled in Rayalseema and married Rukmini Devi the daughter of a very wealthy landlord ie the Palegar or Poligar of Kovelakuntla in 1667, at the age of 21. Vittal died at the age of 54 in 1700 AD because of some ailment and his son Shankar Dev Rao became the zamindar of Mahadevpalli at the age of 32, the year his father died. Shankar Dev Rao who was born in 1668 married Yamini Devi the daughter of the Palegar of Punganuru when he was 20 years old in 1688 and she was 17 years old, their son was born in 1689. Vittal always maintained close ties with the Marathas under Shivaji, then with his son and successor Chatrapathi Sambhaji Bhosale who was beheaded under sordid conditions of brutality by the Mughal forces in 1689, at the orders of the Mughal Emperor Aurangzeb. Vittal's son and successor Shankar Dev Rao carried on with this tradition and maintained close ties with Chatrapathi Sahu or Sambaji-II and the Peshwas who came to head the Marathas after Chatrapathi Sahu or Sambaji Bhosale-ll.

Chapter 4

The Palegars

Rayalseema the land of the Rayas of Vijayanagar fame has always been a land of predators. The word Raya like Raja, Rana indicates feudatory status but the Rayas of Vijayanagar were not feudatories or vassals, they ruled over a substantial portion of the Deccan and neighbouring Tamil speaking areas. The rulers of Vijayanagar never had a centralised armed force, instead they gave powers to small rulers or palegars, who could muster and maintain small private armies and paid taxes to the Vijayanagar Kings and provided the king with their military as and when the necessity arose. The palegars enjoyed autonomy so long as they paid taxes to the Vijayanagar Kings who gave hundreds of acres of land to the palegars. Decentralisation of power was not restricted to the establishment of local rule but it served the purpose of maintaining law and order through a network of palegars. After the fall of the Kingdom of Vijayanagar and the rule of the Rayas of Vijayanagar came to an end following the battle of Talikota in 1565 AD, when the forces of Vijayanagar were defeated by the combined forces of the Bahmani Sultans. A period of anarchy prevailed, thereafter from this anarchy the palegars or polegars of Rayalseema established independant territories. The palegars excersised control over groups of villages, a few hundreds in extent, a rule that amounted to little more than plain plunder by the palegar and his gang of violent casteman (Reddy, Naidu, Velama, Balija, Nayak, Muslim, Boya and those who settled in Rayalseema and married local Telugu speaking women etc) and their followers.

The palegars dictated and maintained dominance with high handedness through armed strength, by suppressing the people who fell under their control without any rule or norm. This suppression went on at the grass root level. On the other hand at the higher level after the fall of Vijayanagar Kings, the power changed from the hands of one Nawab to another. Towards the middle of the 18th century ie 1755 AD, areas of Rayalseema came under Hyder Ali, the Nawab of Mysore, but his son was dispossessed of this region/territory by the Nizam of Hyderabad with the help of the British East India Company. Then some time in 1800 AD the districts of Cuddapah, Kurnool, Ananthapur and Bellary was ceded to the British East India Company and came under the direct rule of the company. However the armed palegars and their factions based on caste lines continued with their age old custom of murder and mayhem sparked by property disputes, illicit contacts with women, including married women turned mistresses, forcible marriage of children and to avenge the murders of their leaders, family members and people belonging to the same caste.

As a result towards the beginning of the 20th century the British rulers under the Crown of England attempted to suppress the palegars by using very harsh methods. The job of suppressing the palegars was given to Thomas Munroe an English officer of the Crown. Thomas Munroe came down with a heavy hand on the palegars and went so far as to publicly hang the then palegar of Kovelakuntla. These coercive methods however did not produce the desired results, the palegars and the thirty thousand force they controlled were beyond control. Under the circumstances, the British did the next best thing they could do and that was to convert the palergars into their allies and refrained from interfering in the the law and order situation in Rayalseema so long as the palegars paid taxes to the British Crown. From that time Rayalseema has remained a land ravaged by rival gangs, faction fighting and driven by the concept of taking bloody and brutal revenge from generation to generation. The factions/armed gangs are to this day involved in illicitt activities such as smuggling of forest produce, growing and supplying opium and distilling illicit liquor. The gangs are different from other criminal gangs in the sense that they are not made up of professional criminals but by peasants driven by caste based equations. The second reason that binds the gangs is not only pecuniary or other material benefits but also an intense feudal loyalty as a matter of traditional "dharma" to their chieftains or the palegar. Every slight, imagined or real is avenged as viciously as every substantial challenge to the palegar's power, property or prestige. Assault, murder and burning of the rival's houses were the principal methods employed to assert one's power and authority. To this day the Palegars ruthlessly pursue their rivals and pass on the baggage of vengeance to the subsequent generations.

"No one escapes from life alive"

– Michael Crichton

Chapter 5

Tondavada

Some years back I went along with my family consisting of my wife and daughter to visit a relative who lived in Tondavada a village located in the hinterland of a very vast area strewn with rocks, stones and boulders called Rayalseema or Raallaseema in the local language, Telugu. "Raallu" means stones and "seema" means region. This rock and boulder strewn countryside was interspersed occasionally with clusters of greenery near a pond or a well. The type of vegetation was predominantly the xerophytic type such as cactus, thorny shrub jungle with palm trees. Water was extremely scarce and anyone who was going into the hinterland to visit someone stocked up enough water, because if you ran out of water there was no village or hamlet close by to turn to, in fact all the villages were at a very great distance and in many cases there was not even a motorable road leading to those villages. Some villages had been electrified, the rest which included the majority made do with neem oil lit lamp light. Walking around at night was not advisable because of the abundance of scorpions, spiders, millipedes, centipedes and snakes. The most poisonous snakes that roamed this vast hinterland were cobras, kraits and vipers. The biggest of the non poisonous snakes was the rock python measuring 10 to

12 feet in length. The only warm blooded animals were leopards, bears, hyenas, jackals, foxes and rabbits. The birds that lived in this region included weaver birds, swallows, egrets, kingfishers, hawks, eagles and vultures. There was no time of the year when the temperature was anything below 36 to 38 degrees Centigrade. The temperatures in the summer months hovered around 45 degree C ie the weather in this region throughout the year was best described as being hot, hotter and hottest. At night there was a remarkable change, the temperature fell sharply and at times it became icy cold. All in all, those who eked out a living in this place were robust and hard working because if they lacked any one of these qualifications, they did not live very long.

We travelled by an overnight bus from Hyderabad to Madanapalle and arrived by a hired taxi in Molakalachruvu on the highway which cut through this region, which was bounded to the south by very steep hills at a very great distance covered by dense forests. The forested area was in the windward side where there was plenty of rainfall, the rest of the boulder and rock strewn plain area was in the rain shadow area where rainfall was scarce. From Molakalachruvu, we took the dirt road that led to my relative's place "Tondavada", which literally means the abode of the chameleons. While driving on the uneven, muddy road with any amount of stones, cobbles and pebbles, I noticed that the hot air rising from the ground created a peculiar wavy, shimmering pattern as layer after layer of hot air rose above the hot and arid plain on both sides of the road. Through this curtain of hot air I thought I saw what looked like the front portion of a very big mansion, the kind of house in which Zamindars or Doras (landlords who owned very vast areas of land and lived on it in palatial mansions) lived.

Zamindar mansion Mahadevpalli

In India, a zamindar was a holder or occupier(dar) of land (zamin). The roots of this word are Persian and the resulting name was widely used wherever Persian influence was spread by the Mughals or other Indian Muslim dynasties. In Bengal the word denoted a hereditary tax collector who could retain 10 percent of the revenue he collected. In the 18th century the British government in India made zamindars land owners, thus creating a landed aristocracy in Bengal and Bihar that lasted until Indian

Independance in 1947. In parts of north India, especially Uttar Pradesh a zamindar denoted a very large land owner with proprietary rights. In Maratha territories the name was generally applied to all local hereditary revenue officers. In sum and essence, zamindars were large land owners entrusted with the collection of revenue in cash or kind from those who tilled their lands. The zamindars had proprietary rights over the land and the right to collect revenue from those lands could be inherited by his progeny from generation to generation ie the right was hereditary in nature.

I asked the driver whose name was Krishna,"whose house is that, on the horizon?" He pretended not to hear me, so I asked once again "Krishna, who lives in that house over there?", this time he had no choice but to answer me and he said "I do not know, that place is called Mahadevpalli and that house is all that is left to be seen. It was once inhabited by the Zamindar Shankar Dev Rao and his family. A terrible tragedy befell him and his family. The rest of the inhabitants of that place left overnight for some unknown destination. That house has been in existence for a very very long time, some say the house is hundreds of years old, anyway no one goes there." We had driven more than ten to twelve kilometres before we arrived in Tondavada, it was late in the afternoon. My cousin brother Ramesh, a medical compounder was waiting for us eagerly and was delighted to see us. His wife, Kamala, a quiet spoken and homely person welcomed us into their house. The house was very airy and comfortable and both my wife and I spent some time with their children until it was time for dinner. After dinner I took my cousin aside and asked him about the house in Mahadevpalli. My cousin told me what I had already gleamed from the driver Krishna and a few more facts.

According to my cousin a couple of years back a notorious gang of three criminals looted a very rich landlord's house in one of the villages and decamped with a considerable amount of gold and jewellery, the police hunted them down and finally when they had nowhere to go the criminals had taken refuge in the zamindar's vast mansion. The next mornig in broad daylight a very large police party entered the zamindar's mansion, on receiving a tip off that the criminal gang was holed up there. The police party which went into the vast mansion was drawn mainly from people who were born and brought up in and around Rayalseema. They had heard strange stories about this house and were aware that it had a a dark and evil past. They went to investigate because they had been asked by their seniors to do so, left to themselves they may not have ventured into the zamindar's house. But it stands to reason that even when a fairly large posse of policemen entered the mansion they did so with great caution, making sure that they did not disturb anything. They did not force open any door or window that was closed. They avoided the areas inside the mansion where there was dense undergrowth, creepers and wines and they did not attempt to hack their way through the undergrowth using a machete or an aruval. In other words they chose the path of least resistance into the house. When they entered the vast mansion they found to their horror, one member of the gang or at least what was left of him, at the bottom of a very wide staircase. He was probably running for his dear life from something when he tumbled down the staircase and broke his neck. But what was left of him was nothing more than his skull with hair, teeth and the remaining skeleton covered by a sallow, jaundiced skin. It was difficult for the police to believe that this was all that was left of him. The police found the remaining two criminals in a similar condition in one room on the first floor, here ie in this room, there was some sign of a confrontation between the thieves and whoever killed them. The windows showed clear signs that they had been forced open. The question was who forced it open? Did the thieves open the widows to get away or did something else that was on their trail enter that way into the room. It appeared as if their whole body which includes muscles, ligaments, blood and cartilage barring the outer skin and the bones had been dissolved and the life sustaining vigour and vitality, sucked out. There was no sign of any violence except for the corpses and the powerful stench of ammonia that emanated from the puddle of urine in which the remnants of each body was lying. The urine was all that was excreted out by whatever had cosumed them. The police party removed what was left of the three criminals and beat a hasty retreat from that house which they found, had the effect of chilling them to their bones, whatever they had seen and retrieved was good enough for them to make out a report. The remaining part of the report would be filled in, after receiving the forensic report. My cousin had found out all these facts from the sub inspector of police who was incharge of this case and who was a good family friend. The forensic report which was sketchy about the cause of death, mentioned that the urine was probably due to the metabolism of purines in the human body.

A few years later a married man and a married woman took shelter in the mansion to avoid being detected by villagers who had come to know about their illicit relationship. A cowherd saw the couple running into the zamindar's mansion. The villagers reported what they knew and what the cowherd had seen, to the police on the following day. The police swung into action and as in the previous case a search party was organised and the police once again searched the premises without disturbing anything in that house. Finally they found the remnants of both the man and the woman. As in the previous case the victims had been consumed leaving behind their remains in a puddle of urine, but there was a difference, the heads of the victims, which they had covered in cloth gamchas i.e a long piece of cloth, in a vain attempt to fend off their attacker, was intact. What the policemen who saw the heads could not forget was the look of sheer fear and horror imprinted in the eyes of the victims which was vide open. Many members from the police party suffered from recurring nightmares for many nights thereafter. The forenscic report could not once again conclusively prove the cause of death.

That night I slept over whatever information I could collect. The next morning I suggested we should go for shopping in Madanapalle and have lunch there before returning to Tondavada. I requested Ramesh to ask someone who knew Rayalseema to wait for us in Molakalacheruvu to show us around. Ramesh readily agreed and said that his assistant Bilal was the right person for the job. Bilal would be waiting for us to return by around 4 o' clock in the afternoon in Molakalacheruvu. As decided, we finished shopping, had lunch and hired a local taxi in Madanapalle with a driver who was not from Rayalseema but was from some other region to drive us back to Tondavada via Mahadevpalli. Since the driver was a newcomer he had no objection to driving us to Mahadevpalli unlike the previous driver who was reticent to talk about the place, let alone go anywhere near it. On our arrival at Molakalacheruvu we found Bilal waiting for us and as soon as he got into the taxi we drove off. After a while, I indicated the way which went roughly in the direction of Mahadevpalli and the zamindar's mansion which was silhouetted on the horizon.

Finding our way to the zamindar's mansion was not difficult. By around 5 pm in the afternoon we slowly wound our way over the vast muddy, boulder, stone and cobble strewn country side to the entrance of the zamindari property at Mahadevpalli. Right at the entrance was a massive black granite stone arch, the height of the arch at it highest point must have been about twenty five feet above the ground, on either side of this stone arch, supporting it were massive stone pillars which must have measured at least about eighteen feet in height, the stone pillars were completely overrun by a creeper or a vine with long tendrils, very similar to the common money plant except that the leaves were much bigger and the tendrils were very much longer and robust. The creeper added an element of colour, greenery and its flowers added beauty to an otherwise dull and drab countryside. The fragrance exuded by the flowers was divine. I decided that on the way out, I would definitely take a few cuttings of this exquisite plant. The arch was covered upto a certain extent but a major portion of the arch, especially the portion above the gate was not covered by the creeper. Perched on these stone pillars was a pair of grotesque stone gargoyles with wings. The stone pillars supported two very ancient and very heavy wrought iron gates which were also overrun by the same creeper, the height of each gate was about fifteen feet. Extending on either side of the gate was a creeper covered wall with a parallel row of stunted trees with stout trunks, the height of this stone wall was around fifteen feet.

The iron gates were wide open, as if it did not matter who entered. Well ahead of the gate on one side was a massive stone edict embedded in the ground, the above ground portion had a height of about five feet and a width of around three or four feet. Carved on this edict was the palm of a human hand with the fingers held together with red kumkum or vermillion (a red powder which is applied by Indians on their forehead to ward off evil) powder smeared on it, probably the work of a village vagabond, with the words "Thaamba" inscribed below the palm. Because I was acquainted with a number of Indian languages I was able to make out that the word written in Marathi (Marathi is written using Devanagari alphabets which are slightly different from Hindi alphabets) meant STOP, I rolled down the glass windows of the vehicle and carefully read what was inscribed below the word "Thaamba" in Telugu. There was no necessity for me to get down to read what was inscribed on the stone edict because it was close enough for me to reach out and touch it.

It was a hot afternoon and the air conditionining inside our car was running at maximum capacity to ensure that everyone inside the car was comfortable which included the three of us, the driver Suresh and Bilal. As we entered the estate a monitor lizard measuring approximately three to five feet in length from the head to the tip of the tail crossed our path. The driver was driving very slowly and he was able to prevent our vehicle from running over the lizard. We progressed a little further on the road, when in the rays of the setting Sun, we could see the massive outline of the mansion built over 300 years ago by the zamindar Shankar Dev Rao. It must have been built over at least three acres of land and surrounding it, was open land with dry grass, shrubs, dotted with mango, palm trees, and very stout but stunted trees with leaves and flowers similar to the leaves on the vines. The girth of the trees indicated that they must have been a few hundred years old. All of this grew on an area roughly measuring at least a few hundred acres. At that moment I distinctly heard the high pitched cry of a child and looked around to see whether anyone was around with a child but there was no one. Nothing grew on this open space in front of the house except for small stunted trees from which at close quarters I noticed the vines emerged, many more monitor lizards scurried past our vehicle. It was quite evident that this house did not have a visitor for a very very long time, the lizards were used to living there without any kind of hindrance or threat from anyone.

I noticed that Bilal inspite of the airconditioning was looking very sick and I also noticed that he was sweating profusely. By this time we were in front of the mansion, it was truly a majestic building with high colonnades of Corinthian pillars, a beautiful fountain in front and a very imposing frontage. The main door which was made of very old wood, probably teak wood was wide open. All of this and the walls of this massive mansion were covered by the same beautiful creeper or vine that covered the gates and the perimeter walls. We were about half a kilometre from the mansion when I decided that we should walk the rest of the way to the open doorway of the mansion at the end of approximately four flights of stairs. I rolled down my window, the fragrance in the air was not just divine, it was intoxicating and enticing. I once again heard a child crying followed by someone calling out. I was certain the mansion was inhabited. I thought some poor beggar and his family was staying in it and it was their child that I heard crying.

At this point our escort Bilal with great difficulty told me "Sahab, please turn back, it will be dark soon." I said "yes, we will just look around as long as there is sunlight, and then we will get back." Bilal said "Sahab, please in the name of Allah, let us leave this place without any delay." I was getting irritated, so I snapped at Bilal "what is wrong with you." Bilal said "this place reeks of evil." I looked at Bilal and choosing my words carefully I asked him "what do you know about this place or about this house which you are not telling me?" Bilal said "Sahab, all I know is that there are no villages within a vicinity of ten kilometers from this place, the villagers in this place as you know are extremely poor and live in small shacks made of stone and slate. They could have pulled down this building and used the stone and the teak wood to construct their houses but they did not do that. Infact they do not bring their cattle or goats to graze within five kilometres of this place." I said "Bilal, your story is interesting, but it may be that the poor, uneducated villagers are superstitious and there is really no cause for concern." Bilal said "no", with finality and then he continued "sahab, did you read the inscription on the stone tablet at the entrance," I said "I read Thaamba was inscribed on the edict which means stop in Marathi." Bilal said "sahab, you obviously did not get the full meaning of what else was written on that tablet." The meaning of the other words on that tablet means "do not enter" in Telugu, the combined meaning is "stop, do not enter." I said "oh, why not, what is the problem, who is going to stop me."

Bilal said "no one will stop you, all I know is that whatever is in there, feeds on warm blooded animals." My wife who was patiently hearing this conversation intruded to say "let us go back", and then she asked Bilal "do you know anyone who knows the history of this place?" Bilal said "yes, my great grandfather who stays in Gudupalli and is over 100 years old may be in a position to answer some of your questions, because despite his age he is fit as a fiddle and his mind is razor sharp." We decided to go back, on the way out I wanted to take a few cuttings of the creeper but my wife dissuaded me from doing so, on the the grounds that we would come back in broad daylight and collect any number of cuttings. While driving out of the main gate in the dim evening light before it became totally dark, I noticed a dozen vultures perched on the stone arch over the gate which was free of creepers, it was distinctly ominous.

The Sun had set, except for the light cast on the road by our vehicle's head lights, there was pitch darkness all around us and a peculiar silence had descended which was akin to the "silence of the graveyard". We arrived at my cousin's place in Tondavada, in pindrop silence. All that we did on the way back was, to drink the cold lassi that my relative had sent along in a flask, along with disposable paper cups.

A couple of days later we went to stay with another relative, my wife's sister Chinnammai who was in charge of a small primary health centre in that village(also catered to a dozen surrounding villages) and her son Sivarama in Gudupalli, where incidentally Bilal's grandfather was also staying.

Painting: Abode of the Vedagiri Narsimhaswamy

Chapter 6

A visit to Gudupalli

We arrived in Gudupalli at 8 am in an autorickhaw after leaving Tondavada at 6 am in the morning. My wife's sister and her son were waiting for us. The house in which they lived, belonged to a zamindar whose great grand children had moved on. There was no living member from the zamindar's descendants living in any portion of that house.The first thing I noticed was the massive, ornately designed teak wood doors, the height of each door was about 12 feet and the width was about 8 feet. The doors had brass door knobs and other decorations which in the good old days would have been made to shine, now no one cared to polish them. This door led to a small corridor which in turn opened into a vast durbar hall. The walls of this room must have been about 25 feet high, the length about 80 feet and the width about 40 ft. At one end of this room was a raised platform which was as wide as the room, only the length was about 20 feet, the height of this platform would have been about 6 feet and there was a flight of stairs on either side, which one had to climb to get on to this raised platform. In olden days the zamindar was seated on a thick mattress covered with a white cotton cloth on this raised platform.

On the walls on three sides of this raised platforms or dias, were displayed very ancient portrait paintings of the 10 generations of zamindars in royal regalia, wearing traditional headgear and a variety of gold jewellery studded with diamonds, rubies, emeralds and other precious stones. The predecessors of the last incumbent had stayed in this vast house and over a period of time, their progeny shifted to the cities of Andhra Pradesh where they had thriving businesses. The remaining walls of the durbar hall, leaving the portion around the raised dias, were adorned with animal trophies such as the heads of tigers, leopards, bears, bison and a variety of deer that the zamindars had hunted and killed over the years, while engaging in their favourite passtime which was hunting or shikar. The walls were also adorned with a variety of spears, swords, shields, axes, daggers, matchlock and flintlock muskets, muzzle loaded smooth bore guns.

Hunting Trophies

At other times the zamindars spent their time in the company of their concubines or watching a dance or natch girls performing along with their family members or in the company of their guests. On such occasions the women folk who rarely if ever came out in public, viewed the dance or any other function seated behind a veiled curtain on the terrace, towards the rear of the house ie in zanana behind a purdah, which ensured that the women of the household could watch the performance, without anyone from the crowd below being able to see them (purdah is a system which keeps a woman secluded in a seperate part of the house behind a veiled curtain, the literal meaning of the word zanana is "of the women" or "pertaining to women". It contextually refers to the part of a house belonging to a Hindu or a Muslim family in South Asia, which is reserved for the women of the household. The zanana is the inner part of the house in which only women lived, where only close family members could enter. The outer part of the house such as the durbar hall was exclusively for men and was called the mandana). Almost all zamindars spent some portion of their time dispensing justice, settling disputes and in matters relating to revenue collection from the villages that fell under their zamindari.

(**Historical perspective in case of Muslim rulers**: In the case of Nizams, sultans, nawabs and Muslim zamindars apart from zanana and purdah in which they kept their womenfolk as Niccalao Mnucci put it, "the muslim rulers were very fond of women, who were the principal relaxation and almost the only pleasure". The large size of the harem was dictated by a number of factors such as marriage and war. Many prisoners of war entered the harem along with slaves. A large number of women servants came as part of the Dover, when a Nizam or a sultan or a nawab married the daughter of a local ruler or a zamindar. Before the 16th century, tradition held that the wife of a sultan or a nawab was allowed to give birth to only one son ie one male child, if she had daughters she could have sexual relations with the sultan until she had a male child. This ensured that each potential sultan or nawab had the full maternal attention and this also ensured that no wife or concubine became more important or more powerful than the others. In the coming centuries this tradition was diluted which in turn led to internecine quarrels between siblings).

(**Historical perspective in case of Hindu Rajas and zamindars:** There are two kinds of marriages among the Marathas one in which the tali is tied round the neck of the bride by the bridegroom whose full wife she then became, the other in which the tali is tied to a sword, a ceremony which makes the woman a permanent concubine of the man. Dharmavalli Bai one of Serfoji's twenty six sword wives said that a sword was placed and homam was performed and she came round the homam while the men chanted mantras. After she had prostrated herself before the Maharaja, he tied the tali. She said that seven or eight women were married at the same time and all were married in the same fashion with the placing of the sword. It is significant that there is no mention of the giving of the bride to the bridegroom ie Kanyadanam, an essential feature of every valid Hindu marriage. In another case a dagger was used instead of a sword. In another instance the Zamindar of Saptur who was the bridegroom was of the Kumbla caste, while the bride was of Vellala caste. Both these are subdivisions of the same Sudra caste, but a dagger was used instead of the sword during the marriage to indicate the inferiority of the bride's status. The tali or bottu was tied in the presence of the dagger, the dagger being placed to represent the zamindar who did not attend in person. The woman was the wife of the zamindar, but inferior in status to the "patni" wife. The dagger marriage was held to be analogous to an anuloma marriage, that is, a marriage between a man of a higher caste and a woman of a lower caste. The sword wives of the late Raja Shivaji were drawn from several castes, different from the Raja's caste, there were Marathas, Sudras, Iyengars, Christians, however none of them was a Brahmin woman. In 1899 while adjudicating on a suit brought by a reversioner, the Subordinate Judge of Kumbakonam found that there was no such form of marriage as a sword marriage which is recognized in Hindu Law and that Radha Bai was not the lawfully wedded wife of Pratap Singh but only his concubine and her daughter's son was not a reversioner but the child of an illegitimate mother. Two witnesses examined at the trial stated that the bride held the tip of the sword while the bridegroom held the handle and in that state they went round the sacred fire in the palace and that tying of tali, taking seven steps, homam and other ceremonies were performed simultaneously. The Pundit declared that the sword marriage was a Gandharva form of marriage peculiar to Kshatriyas ie the warrior caste, the distinctive feature of Gandharva marriage being that there is no giving away of the bride. In order to constitute a lawful marriage among Hindus, it is essential that certain nuptial rites should be performed, otherwise the marriage is only a Gandharva marriage, or, as it is described in Brindavana v. Radhamani (1889) I.L.R., 12 Mad., 72 at p. 75, "a marriage importing an amorous connection founded on reciprocal desire".)

Next to this durbar hall on one side were two rooms ie on the side opposite the dias ie the raised platform, each room measured 20 feet in width and 20 feet in length, the height of the walls in both the rooms was the same as the wall height in the hall, both the rooms had windows, both rooms were interconnected and also had a door which led to the mainhall. In these rooms the munshi ie "clerk or secretary", the writer ie "native Indian who was capable of writing in the local language as well as in English" and other staff members who were connected with revenue collection and maintenance of records were seated on thick mattresses spread on the floor and covered with a white cotton spread.

18th century Munshi

The first floor ie the floor above the main hall and the adjacent two rooms was upheld by multiple horizontal iron beams which ran from the rear wall to the front wall. The rear wall had a small door which led to a massive kitchen measuring about 40 feet in length and 15 feet in width, the height of the walls was the same as the walls in the main hall. In this kitchen at times food was prepared for dozens of people on vast wood fired stoves in massive bronze vessels by half a dozen kansamas or cooks. Next to the kitchen was an open space with a door leading to a vast courtyard and a small flight of stairs leading to the first floor. At one end of the courtyard close to the small shed in which goats and a very large shed where cows were kept, was the stone pillar to which defaulters were tied and flogged, some of whom died because they were unable to withstand the pain.

18th century Native Writer

Beyond this open space adjacent to the kitchen, was the armoury, a room measuring about 30 feet in length and 15 feet in width. It goes without saying that the height of the walls in all the rooms was the same as the height of the walls in the durbar hall. The courtyard which lay beyond was about 800 feet by 80 feet. It was bounded on one side by a double storey building which housed the household staff, bodyguards and their families, at the farthest end by a large cowshed, a smaller goat shed and a wrought iron gate which was locked, if opened this gate served as a rear exit. Opposite this cow shed in the middle of this courtyard was a raised mandap or a stage (with four small, very heavy, ancient cannons at the four corners of the base, along with a small mound of iron cannon balls) on which in ancient days devdasis or natch girls (dancing girls and courtesans) danced for the merriment of the zamindar and his family. Closer to the house on the third side of this courtyard there was a series of three separate toilets and three separate bathrooms, meant to be used by the zamindar's close family members. Each bathroom had an inbuilt copper vessel or undal which could be heated using pieces of wood and twigs from the outside, inside the bathroom was a small stone tank which held cold water, this tank was kept filled by servant women. A person was expected to take the hot water from the copper vessels in a bucket and add cold water from the stone tank so as to bring down the temperature and bathe in it. The bathrooms were well ventilated, which is how it was supposed to be as per vastu and a portion was kept open to the sky, while taking a bath one could simultaneously enjoy the warmth of the Sun's rays, a gentle breeze or the beauty of a moonlit and star studded sky. It is ironic that in present times the same is being offered by some heritage hotels and resorts as a part of their luxury package. In addition to this, one stone slab on the floor was selectively placed, that had rough surface and was meant to be used as a pumice stone, for rubbing one's feet to remove dead skin. I wonder how thoughtful it was of them to have conceived all of this in those days, which people in the present day refer to as those backward and dark times.

On the first floor there were three rooms. The first room must have measured about 20 feet in length and 40 feet in width, then there was a corridor measuring abot 10 feet in length and about 40 ft in width, the doors of the first bedroom opened into the corridor, the corridor connected with the staircase and opened into a terrace of about 80 feet in length and 15 feet in width facing the rear of the house on which female members of the zamindar's family sat and watched a dance or anything else that was performed on the mandap or the raised platform in the middle of the courtyard.. The doors and windows had intricate wood carvings. The verandah railings and arches were decorated with wrought iron frames, fitted with colored glass pieces. The grills still showed the images of Radha and Krishna engraved on it in the center. The second and the third bedroom were interconnected and both opened into the corridor, each room was 25 feet in length and 40 feet in width. The second bedroom opened onto a 20 feet by 40 feet terrace.The height of the walls in all the first floor rooms was 15 feet and multiple iron girders running horizontally from wall to wall upheld the roof of the first floor. From the corridor there was a flight of stairs leading to the second floor. The second floor had only two rooms measuring about 25 feet in length and 40 feet in width, the height of the walls was approximately 12 feet, the remaining space measuring 30 feet by 40 feet though roofed in was open ie with no walls, from the second floor there was a short flight of stairs to the terrace which was 80 feet in length by 40 feet in width ie the same dimension as the main hall. The zamindar's house had three terraces which gave a grand stand view of the surrounding fields growing sunflowers, mountains in the distance and a lake was visible at a very great distance.

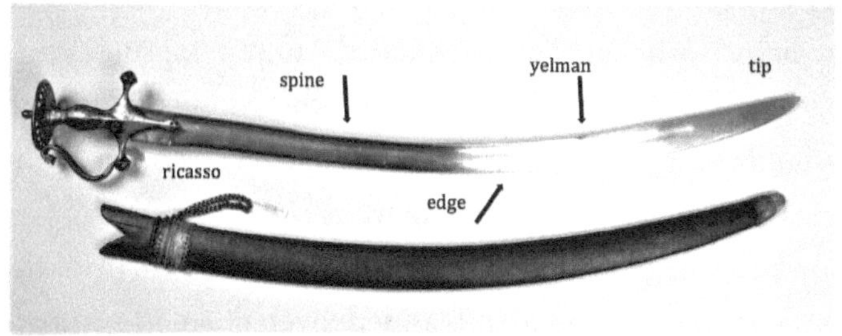

Ancient Sword

Those who wanted something or had something to say, sat on the mattress spread on the floor in front of the dais. They would be called one by one, by the zamindar's attendant by name, then without their headgear with their hands folded in front and without making eye contact, they approached the dias on which the zamindar was seated and stated whatever they had on their mind. The zamindar would agree, not agree or give time for the person concerned to make amends. However if the concerned person did not make amends by way of making the necessary payment or in some other form within the time period as stipulated by the zamindar, he or she would be taken to the rear of the house and tied to the stone pillar, stripped off their clothing, then depending on the quantum of punishment decided by the zamindar in terms of the number of lashes to be given, the defaulter would be given a lashing with a leather whip. At other times the punishment was far more severe and involved being beaten and made to starve for days on end. In the case of females stripping and parading them naked in villages was common. Sometimes the zamindar took a fancy to a particular female defaulter, in such cases she would be escorted to one of the rooms above and would be ravished by the zamindar for as long as he pleased irrespective of her marital status. This went on for a couple of days or a few months or at times until the woman became pregnant and delivered an illegitimate child. However no one spoke about such women and their progeny for fear of inviting the zamindar's wrath. The poor victims at times succumbed to their injuries and died due to the sexual excesses inflicted on them that however did not bother the zamindar in any way whatsoever.

After looking around the empty house of the zamindar, we decided to retire to our room ie one of the two rooms adjacent to the main hall. After some time Bilal came to inform us that his great grandfather was not keeping well and was advised to take three days bed rest. There was nothing much to be done in Gudupalli, so in the intervening three days along with Bilal we decided to explore the country side. On the first day, I and Sivarama, my wife's nephew, decided to scout around the neighbouring areas. We went past a number of sunflower fields and climbed a small mountain which gave a grandstand view of the country side which for the greater part consisted of rocky patches interspersed with small fields of sunflowers for miles together, going as far as a series of steep mountains almost on the horizon with a village in the great distance which Sivarama called "Cheruvukindapalli". We sat on this rocky mountain and I shared a couple of my cigarettes with a few shepherds. The shepherds cautioned us against leopards and bears which lurked on these rocky hills, caves and promontories especially after darkness fell. Finally after viewing the countryside to our heart's content we decided to get back, it was very hot. On the way back we came across a fairly wide, solitary slab of stone placed on a raised mound beneath a tamarind tree. We decided to lie down on this stone and sleep for a while. A gentle breeze was blowing which made us feel sleepy. After about an hour or so we awoke and saw about half a dozen villagers watching us with great interest. One of them said "sleep, sleep, there is no problem, they are good people", Sivaram asked the villager "who are you referring to?", he replied "the husband and wife pair sleeping beneath the stone slab". That was when it struck us that, what we mistook for an ordinary slab of rock, was in fact a plain slab of rock, placed over the graves of a couple who had died many years ago. It did not take us a second longer to get off the stone slab and after reaching home we both bathed before having our dinner and we made plans to visit the village of Sompalyam, a village with great archaeological significance, on the following day. That night after dinner we all sat on charpoys placed on the second floor terrace under a brilliant star lit night. We could see clearly billions of stars, in the absence of any dust or any other kind of industrial pollution that clogged up the night sky above most cities. In Gudupalli there was no such problem, the air was pure and we took in lung fulls of that clear, fresh air, it had a peculiar refreshing quality about it. We could hear intermittently the strains of a bhajan coming from a temple located in a distant village. During the day it was hot outside, but inside the zamindar's house because of the high walls it was always cool. At night there was a drastic drop in temperature and at times it became chilly and cold. The next morning we awoke and strolled around on the terrace taking in the early morning countryside and saw the Sun rise from behind a series of mountains to the east of the zamindar's house. Then we saw millions of sunflowers open in the direction of the rising sun, it was an unforgettable sight along with myriad butterflies in a variety of colors, hues and shades, we had never seen so many butterflies and that too in so many colors in a single place. The chilly early morning air was a welcome change from the smoke ridden polluted air that we breathed in our cities. We saw a large Lotus pond to the west of the house and a temple to the north. A shepherd brought two baby goats, along with newly hatched ducklings for my daughter to play with. My daughter had a whale of a time playing with the ducklings and the baby goats until we had our breakfast, then we decided to go by a state transport bus to Sompalyam.

After boarding the bus my daughter suddenly screeched like an owl. The bus driver fearing that a child had fallen off the bus brought the bus to a halt, I asked my daughter "why did you screech like that?" Without batting an eye lid she said "daddy my cap flew off through the open window and has fallen on the road". A lot of people on the bus laughed and we waited until my wife's nephew Sivarama fetched my daughter's cap which as she said was lying on the road. Then once again the bus started and we were dropped off in Sompalyam. In Sompalyam we made our way to the Shri Chennakesava temple built by a local chieftain, then by the Cholas and later developed by the Vijayanagara kings. The temple is in ruins currently and is being maintained by the Archaeological Society of India. As soon as we entered the temple through the main gopuram we saw a chariot carved out of granite which can be seen only in Hampi, the capital of the Vijaynagara kingdom which was ravaged, pillaged and burnt after their forces were defeated in the battle of Talikota in 1565 AD by the combined forces of the Deccan Sultanate, the Golkonda and the Bahmani sultans and their King Alia Rama Raya, a great Hindu King and Statesman, the son-in-law of Emperor Krishna Deva Raya, the founder of the Aravidu dynasty (the fourth and last dynasty of the empire) who was betrayed by two of his trusted muslim commanders, was captured while leading the Vijayanagara forces into battle and beheaded by Hussain Nazim Shah the Nizamshah of Ahmednagar. The Kalyana mantapa in the south west corner ie the raised and covered dais where marriages are performed, had exquisitely carved pillars out of black soapstone and the one thing which characterizes Vijayanagara temples such as this temple was the presence of musical pillars which make a distinct sound when it is tapped. The stone columns, the brackets and the doorways were carved with miniature figures, animals and scrollwork. The temple was a repository of paintings depicting episodes from the epic Ramayana. From this temple the remnants of a fort that existed centuries ago could be seen on the nearby mountain. After looking around the temple, we sat on a lawn surrounding the temple and ate the packed lunch that we brought along. Then we got a lift on someone's jeep till Molakalacheruvu. Here we booked a taxi to take us to Horsley Hills or Horsley konda or Yenugula Mallanna Konda (named after a young girl who according to folklore was reared by elephants and could cure people's ailments, then one day she disappeared, since then she is worshipped as a Goddess and there is a temple atop the hill in her honour), a beautiful hill station near by and to bring us back to Gudupalli. We drove up Horsley hills with cool breeze hitting our face, the hill is named after W H Horsley a British Civil Servant who built a bungalow on that hill in 1862 to escape the scorching heat of the plains, which till to date exists as the Forest Bungalow. The day temperature in Horsley hills can go up to 32 degrees celsius during the summer months but the night temperature can dip to a chilly 10 degrees celsius. Rishi Valley School, a boarding school on Horsley hills founded by Sri Jiddu Krishnamurthi the philosopher is another draw. The abundance of sandal wood, red sanders, eucalyptus, silver oak, mahogany, jacaranda, allamanda and gulmohar coupled with the rich bird life which includes the yellow throated bubul, the red throated flycatcher, the blue headed rock thrush and the ultramarine flycatcher, to name just a few makes Horsley hills a nature lover's paradise. In the hills close to Horsley hills you can find porcupines, sambar deer, cheetal, wild boars, sloth bears and leopards. Catching a glimpse of these animals is easy, especially if you are on a trek. From atop Horsley hills the surrounding terrain is beautiful yet bleak.

Built around Horsley's bungalow is the environmetal centre which is basically a park. At the entrance is a zoo with a modest collection of animals such as deer, bears, rabbits, peacocks etc. To the south of Horsley hills is a view point from where you can see Madanapalle. Next to the Bungalow built by Horsley is a 150 year old eucalyptus tree called the Kalyani tree. To the western side of Horsley hills is a large rocky slope which descends gently. This place is called the Horsley hills view point because it gives a grand stand view of the surrounding country side and the plains below stretching as far as the horizon. Rugged hills and stony plains stretch as far as the eye can see, cool climate and the view make it a great place to relax.

Thereafter we moved to another location about which we had heard a lot, from a distance Gurramkonda looks like a mammoth hill consisting of a single monolithic chunk of rock. The entrance to the fort at the top of this hill is near Ragini Mahal, a pathway leads from the palace to the top of Gurramkonda. As you walk along the path you will come across ancient gates and several layers of fortifications and battlements. The fort atop Gurramkonda has a few water reservoirs, dilapidated bastions, armories and barracks populated by snakes and rabbits. The view from the top of the fort is spectacular. After exploring Horsley hills we had lunch at the APTDC Haritha Hill Resort, we booked a room so that we could use the bathroom and the toilet and take a short nap in the afternoon before returning in our taxi to Gudupalli. By the time we returned to Gudupalli it was well past 8 o' clock at night. To my daughter's delight, the Kirana shop owner at a short distance from our place in Gudupalli had delivered a few water cooled Fanta bottles for my daughter to drink. Since the power supply in Gudupalli was frequently interrupted and erratic, the village folk had learnt to innovate and use a large earthenware pot filled with water to keep anything cool ranging from milk packets to cool drinks.

The next day ie on the fourth day of our stay in Gudupalli we could meet Abdul Razak Khan, Bilal's great grandfather late in the evening. His house was about half a dozen houses away from the zamindar's house in which my sister-in-law was living as a tenant. Abdul Khan was close to or just above a 100 years old but as we were told by Bilal, he was a in fine fettle and on the day we met him, he was in a jovial frame of mind, after exchanging pleasantries we broached the subject concerning the strange events that took place in the zamindar's mansion in Mahadevpalli. Unlike the others Abdul Razak Khan did not show any fear nor was he reticent to talk about Mahadevpalli. Slowly as was his style he spoke at length about what happened over two hundred years ago as he remembered from what his own grandfather had told him when he was a young lad of about 25 years. Then he made a startling revelation, he said "my grandfather told me that his great grand ancestor, someone called Anwar Khan was a bodyguard of the zamindar of Rajanpalli (the father-in- law of Lakshmi Devi, daughter of Vikram Dev Rao and grand daughter of Shankar Dev Rao, zamindar of Mahadevpalli). According to Abdul Razak Khan one night Vikram Dev Rao (the son of zamindar Shankar Dev Rao of Mahadevpalli) came to Rajanpalli with his wife, attendants, workers and bodyguards, after leaving his house under unnatural circumstances. Subsequently he was seen hand writing a very lengthy document sitting late into the night in lamp light, it took him several nights to complete the document. He wrote only at night after ensuring that there was no one around to disturb him or to read what he had written. After several days of this nocturnal exercise he finished the document and then in his own hand writing made an exact copy, both of which he placed in two separate camphor wood boxes. One original copy of this lengthy, hand written, scrolled document he gave the zamindar of Rajanpalli his maternal uncle and the other original he carried with him which it is rumored on his death bed, he gave his son Surya Dev Rao. On reading this document which was a kind of will, declaring that henceforth the zamindari of Mahadevpalli would come under the zamindar of Rajanpalli (ie his daughter's father-in-law), the zamindar of Rajanpalli turned pale and his hands shook violently, thereafter his attendants had to assist him to lie down on his bed. Even in that condition Jaganmohan Dev Rao the zamindar of Rajanpalli forbade anyone from touching or reading the document that was entrusted to him by Vikram Dev Rao.

A few days later the zamindar of Rajanpalli accompanied by his most trusted body guards (Abdul Razak Khan's great grand ancestor Anwar Khan was one of them) and aides, went to the temple of the Goddess Sri Sivagama Sundari Amman, where, after speaking to the head priest or poojari for quite some time, he handed over the camphor wood box which contained Vikram Dev Rao's original, lengthy, hand written and scrolled document. According to Abdul Razak Khan based on what his grand father had narrated to him, his grandfather's great grand ancestor ie Anwar Khan, overheard Jaganmohan Dev Rao, the zamindar of Rajanpalli telling the head priest of the temple that the document that he ie Jaganmohan Dev Rao had entrusted to the head priest's care must not be opened and if for any purpose it is opened then it must not be opened before at least three generations had passed after his ie Jaganmohan Dev Rao's death. According to Abdul, the present head priest of that temple was a direct descendant of the head priest to whom the camphor wood box containing the document was entrusted centuries ago and there was a possibility that the present incumbent may be still in possession of the box with the document.

A few days later we called on the head priest of the Sri Sivagama Sundari Amman temple, after doing our pooja we were introduced to the head priest or the head poojari by a reliable and a well known person in Rayalaseema. The head priest received us and agreed to look for the box if it was still there in his house, he however was not aware that there was any such box with an ancient document in his custody. After a few days we received a message from the head priest that he had located a box, which from its appearance, according to him looked very old, the box had a pair of serpents carved on it. He wanted us to come to his house right away and be present when the box was opened, because he was apprehensive about opening it alone by himself. The same day, we all went to the house of the head priest and after having a cup of tea, the head priest placed a very old camphor wood chest on the table, with great difficulty we managed to pry open the lock. Inside the wooden chest was a document which was written on ancient hand made paper in the form of a very lengthy scroll. The scrolled document was written in Marathi. We could have attempted to read it, but to read, study and to understand the contents in the right context would have taken us a very long time. Under the circumstances there was nothing to be done except to send word to Bilal to come to the priest's house and to translate the document. In the meanwhile since it was closing in on lunch time, the head priest asked us to join him and his wife for lunch, we had a pure vegetarian lunch. After lunch Bilal arrived and it took him several hours to painstakingly translate the document. Finally we knew the dreadful truth and the sequence of events that had taken place in the zamindar's mansion in Mahadevpalli on that fateful night when, Vikram Dev Rao (the son of zamindar Shankar Dev Rao of Mahadevpalli) came to Rajanpalli with his wife, attendants, workers and bodyguards, after leaving his house under unnatural circumstances and in the months preceding that night. We also knew the terrible secret that Vikram Dev Rao carried to his grave. We could understand why the zamindar of Rajanpalli reacted in the manner he reacted after reading the contents of the scrolled document and we knew why he did not keep the document with him but entrusted it to the care of the head priest of the Sri Sivagama Sundari Amman temple. It was the only document that spoke about Malli, what she told Vikram Dev Rao on that terrible night and the secret that they carried to their grave and spelt out the reason why Vikram Dev Rao decided to abandon the zamindar's mansion in Mahadevpalli, once and for all times to come.

The contents of this novel ie Thaamba, is based on the document which remained unread in a camphor wood chest in the possession of the head priests of the Sri Sivagami Sundari AmmanTemple for nine generations from the time it was entrusted to their great, great grand ancestor for safe keeping centuries ago. Apart from the document, other pieces of information in this novel was obtained from the Vamsacharitram ie a detailed family record maintained over generations, spanning several centuries of the Chandragiri, the Venkatagiri and the Pithapuram Royal Families. The descendant of Vikram Dev Rao ie the present zamindar of Dholapur refused to comment on the existence of such a document and a sealed chamber somewhere in the underground portion of Dholapur house. He however did not deny the existence of the document nor did he deny the existence of a sealed chamber with a trunk holding an ancient and diabolical secret.

Chapter 7

The Zamindar's Family

Vittal Dev Rao a senior senani ie soldier, in the Maratha chieftain Chatrapati Shivaji's army, married Rukmini Devi a local telugu woman from a prominent family ie the daughter of the palegar of Kovelakuntla.

Shankar Dev Rao (Pedda Dora), the son of Vittal Dev Rao and the zamindar of Mahadevpalli. Yamini Devi (Pedda Dorasani), wife of the Shankar Dev Rao and daughter of the palegar of Ponganuru.

Vikram Dev Rao (Dora), elder son of the Shankar Dev Rao & Yamini Devi. Maheshwari Devi (Dorasani), wife of Vikram Dev Rao and daughter of the palegar of Bangarupalem.

Bukka Dev Rao (Dora) half brother of Vikram, son of the zamindar Shankar Dev Rao & his second wife Kanta Devi who expired a few years after Bukka's birth. Parvathi Devi (Dorasani), wife of Bukka Dev Rao and daughter of the palegar of Gandikota.

Surya Dev Rao (Chinna Dora), elder son of Vikram Dev Rao & Maheshwari Devi. Lakshmi Devi (Chinna Dorasani), daughter of Vikram Dev Rao & Maheshwari Devi, engaged to Arjun Dev Rao.

Rudra Dev Rao (Chinna Dora) son of Bukka Dev Rao & Parvathi Devi.

Jaganmohan Dev Rao (Pedda Dora), The zamindar of Rajanpalli, son of the Palegar of Ponganuru and younger brother of Yamini Devi, wife of Zamindar Shankar Dev Rao.

Bhramaramba Devi (Pedda Dorasani), wife of Jaganmohan Dev Rao and daughter of the palegar of Penukonda. Arjun Dev Rao (Chinna Dora), son of Jaganmohan Dev Rao.

Raja Shri Vijaya Rama Rao, Raja of Chandragiri, Rani Durga Devi of Chandragiri and elder sister of Yamini Devi the wife of Shankar Dev Rao, zamindar of Mahadevpalli, Shri Gopinatha Venkata Rao, son and crown prince of Chandragiri, Savithri Devi daughter and princess of Chandragiri married to Shri Veera Bhadra Naidu, crown prince of Venkatagiri.

Raja Shri Harishcandra Naidu, Raja of Venkatagiri, Rani Sumathi Devi of Venkatagiri, Shri Veera Bhadra Naidu, crown prince of Venkatagiri.

Raja Shri Devarakonda Vittal Dev Rao, Raja of Bobbili, brother-in-law of Raja Shri Harishchandra Naidu (married to Raja Shri Harishchandra Naidu's sister Meenakshi Devi, Rani of Bobbili).

Servants working in the household of zamindar Shankar Dev Rao:

Mallanna (cook) and his wife Chellammma (household help), Mandanna (cook) and his wife

Lalitamma (household help), Sivasami (cook) and his wife Sundaramma, Pandusami (cook).

Pichiah (gardener) and his wife Kavita (servant), Venkatesan (gardener) and his wife Pachaiyamma, Murugesan (gardener).

Satya Raju (household help) and his wife Ishwari, Maya (grown up daughter of Satya Raju & Ishwari, in an amorous relationship with Rudra Dev Rao).

Cattle Grazers: Rajanna and his wife Bullemma (household help), Bullemma in an amorous relationship with Bukka Dev Rao. Naarappa (cattle grazer) and his wife Akkamma (servant), Munuswamy (cattle grazer) and his wife Kannamma (servant).

Body guards of the zamindar : Ugrasena, Raktha Beeja, Sattenna, Kaalabhairava, Munikanna, Ramu, Gopanna,Vema Reddy, Naagamma, Vishwanatha, Sevappa, Pasupati, Rajagopala, Venkat Reddy and others.

Haribabu and Shanta, who looked after the zamindar's mango orchards, in Vadamalpet along with other workers.

Other people involved

Kirana shop owner in Nagepalli: Kishtiah, Yellamma wife of Kishtiah, Kumi daughter of Kishtiah & Yellamma, who married Vamsi but was deflowered by Bukka Dev Rao on her marital night.

Kirana shop owner in Sompalli: Purniah, Lalitamma wife of Purniah, Vamsi son of Purniah & Lalitamma, who married Kumi and settled for a gold coin for allowing his wife to be deflowered by Bukka.

The outsiders

An unmarried couple claiming to be from the Surya Samrajyam or the Kingdom of the Sun God, Muthu, a married man in a relationship with Malli.

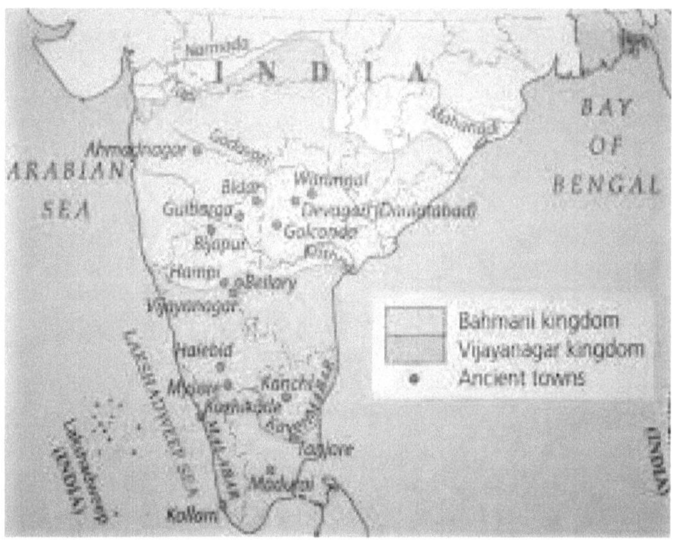

Map showing the extent of the Vijayanagar Empire & the Decccan Sultanate

The battle of Talikota & the Chandragiri Royal Family (the early years when the Rayas ruled Chandragiri):

Chandragiri is historically importantant because of its connection to the 4TH and the last of the Vijayanagar dynasties called the Aravidu dynasty beginning with Alia

Rama Raya the son-in-law of Emperor Krishna Deva Raya who led the forces of Vijayanagar into the battle of Talikota or Tallikotai in 1565 AD and was defeated by the combined forces of the Bijapur Sultanate under the Sultan Ali Adil Shah, the forces of Ahmednagar under Hussein Nizam Shah, the Golkonda forces under Adil Qutub-ul-Mulk and the forces of Bidar under Ibrahim Qutub Shah.

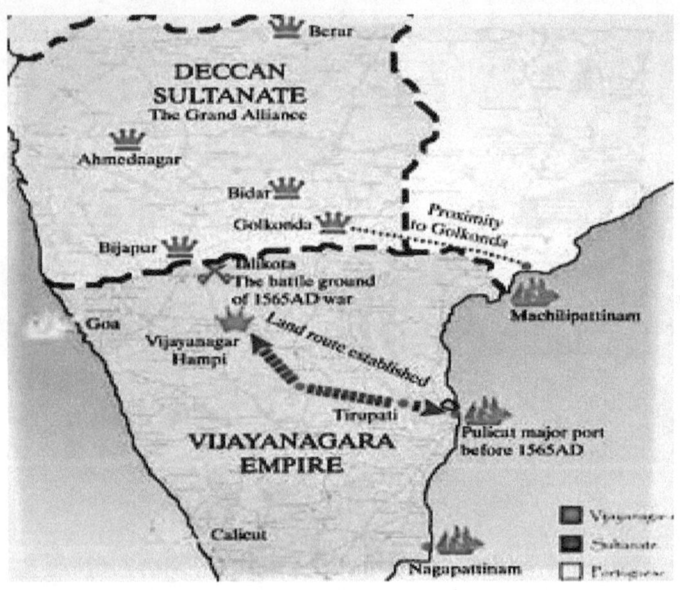

The exact location where the battle of Talikota was fought in 1565 AD

Alia Rama Raya depended on his antiquated elephants. His vast infantry had no body armour and fought dressed only in turbans and loin cloth, with short spears and swords. The cavalry consisted of small country bred ponies, which did not have the strength and the mobility of the Arab steeds used by the opponents. The clincher however lay in the artillery. Although Alia Rama Raya had 200 cannons, they were a generation behind the 600 latest cannons which his opponents had, manned by Turkish and Persian Gunners. Alia Rama Raya was in his 70s and so were his brothers and generals, though they led from the front, they did not have the energy and the vigour to win the battle. The last straw on the camel's back was the betrayal of Alia Rama Raya's own Muslim generals, who at the last minute went over to the enemy.

The main battle took place on 23rd Jan 1565, in a wide area, south of the Krishna River between the villages of Tangadgi and Rakshasi. Alia Rama Raya had deployed his forces with himself in the centre, his brothers Tirumala Deva Raya and Venkatadri Deva Raya on the right and the left flank. The opposing Sultanate forces were deployed in a classic Turkish formation with a screen of light cavalry ahead, the main force in a defensive layout, light cavalry on the flanks and heavy cavalry in the rear as a reserve. Their artillery consisting of 600 cannons was in the centre so as to bring down the maximum volume of fire. The forces were lined up and neither side was making much headway, when around midday, both Tirumala Deva Raya and his brother Venkatadri launched spirited attacks and pushed back the left flank of the Sultanate armies, but they failed to exploit this gain and soon they themselves were pushed back by a shower of arrows and the nimble cavalry of the sultanate armies who charged, fired and then wheeled away. Venkatadri and his son were wounded, the attack launched by them fizzled out. Seeing that the battle was not going well, Alia Rama Raya decided to launch an all out attack with the bulk of his forces from the centre. The attack was met by the combined fire from 600 sultanate cannons. The cannons were primed and the cannon balls filled with copper, iron metal bits which acted as vicious shrapnel wounded a large number of Alia Rama Raya's infantry. Inspite of the casualties, the attack was making headway, when two of his own top military generals acting on a prearranged signal changed ranks and attacked Alia Rama Raya's forces from behind with around 30 to 40 thousand men. This took the Vijayanagar forces completely by surprise and they broke ranks and fled.

Alia Rama Raya's elephant was hit by a cannon shot and fell to the ground and as he was being carried away on a palkhi, he was overtaken by officers of the Sultanate forces and was beheaded on the instructions of the Nizam Shah of Ahmednagar. Worse was to follow, Alia Rama Raya's brother Tirumala Deva Raya fled to Vijayanagar from the battle field and instead of organizing the defence of the capital, he fled the capital with the royal treasury on 1550 elephants. Three days later, the Sultanate forces landed on the capital ie Vijayanagar. Over a periodof 6 months they ransacked, pillaged, plundered, killed over 50 thousand citizens and burnt it. Vijayanagar ie "The City of Victory" had vanished, what still remains of a great and magnificient empire is, the silence and the ruins of Hampi, which stands as mute spectator, where "the City of Victory" stood in history.

Tirumala Deva Raya and his remaining forces fled to Vellore, Penukonda and Chandragiri where his successors ruled for another 81 years. In 1639 it was from a dependant of the last Aravidu raja that the British East India Company obtained permission to build a fort and trading post in Madraspatnam called Fort St. George. In the succeeding years Chandragiri came under the Sultan of Golkonda in 1646. The Golconda and Bijapur Sultans employed Velama, Kamma and Reddy kings as the rulers of various kingdoms and ordered them to pay the tribute and collect revenue. Thus kingdoms/provinces, also known as Samsthanams or Zamindaris, came into existence.

The Venkatagiri Royal Family: The Venkatagiri palace holds priceless records of the "Vamsacharitram" of the Venkatagiri Rajas right from the time the dynasty was founded by the warrior king Bhetala Naidu beginning in 1195 AD and coming down to the present incumbent, Raja Sri Velugoti Govinda Krishna Yachendra Bahadur,K.C.I.E, A.D.C, belonging to the 29th generation. This apart, a fine collection of swords, shields, a very valuable emerald and the throne of Raja Sri Yerradacha Naidu belonging to the 24th generation is on display.

The Pithapuram Royal Family: A member of this dynasty ie the Venkatagiri Royal family (Velama) at some point of time, migrated to a Godavari district and received a sanad in 1749 from Rustam Khan, a general in the Nizam's army and this led to the creation of the Pithapuram royal family or the Pithapuram Samasthanam. The daughter of Raja Sri Rao Venkata Kumara Mahipathi Surya Rao who ruled from 1885-1964 and Rani Chinnamamba Devi of Kapileshwarapuram (Nuzvid zamimndari), Sita Devi married Shri Rangaiah Appa Rao Bahadur, the zamindar of Vayyuru and bore one son.

Later she met HH Pratap Singh Rao Gaekwad ie the last ruling Maharaja of Baroda, at the Madras horse races in 1943 and married him after divorcing her first husband. At that time the Gaekwad was considered the second richest Prince in India. The newly wedded couple set up their second home in the independant principality of Monaco, on the island of Monte Carlo in the Mediterranean Sea, off the coast of France. The Gaekwad transferred a vast amount of wealth fromthe Baroda treasury including the fabulous pearl carpet, a three strand diamond necklace with the famous Pink Brazilian "Star of the South"(128.80 carats) diamond and the "English Dresden" diamond (78.53 carats). The couple also acquired the "Empress Eugenie" diamond and a Ring with a 30 carat Sapphire that Sita Devi wore to the horse races, she believed it brought her good luck and to those who touched it.

Sita Devi was on very close terms with Princess Niloufer, the daughter of the Caliph of Turkey, who is regarded as the direct successor of the Prophet Mohammed and the daughter-in-law of Mir Osman Ali Khan, the last ruling Nizam of Hyderabad. As a result of this friendship, Sita Devi procured some of the world's costliest diamonds from the Guntur and the Golkonda Diamond Mining Company which was owned by Mir Osman Ali Khan, the Nizam of Hydeabad, who in the 1960s according to the Guinness Book of World Records was the wealthiest man in the world. It may be of interest for the reader to know that the Kohinoor diamond which adorns the Crown of England ie the Crown worn by the Kings and Queens of England over the centuries, was mined from the Golkonda Diamond mines in Hyderabad.

The couple had one son whom they named Sayaji Rao Gaekwad and nicknamed "Prince". Sita Devi divorced the Gaekwad in 1956 but hung on to her exalted title and drove around in a Rolls Royce car which still sported the armorial insignia of the princely state of Baroda. Years later at the age of 40 "Prince" committed suicide and Sita Devi who doted on her son, died of a broken heart four years later in 1969. She was the Maharani of Baroda for 40 years until her death in Paris. In 1994 the fabulous pearl carpet was located in a Geneva vault, it had been sold to an Arab Prince for 31 million dollars and is currently on display at the Museum of Islamic Art, Doha in Qatar inspite of the fact that it was commissioned by a Hindu Maharaja. The "Star of the South" and many other gems belonging to Sita Devi were located with jewellers in Amsterdam.

Painting: The Hunt

Chapter 8

Shikar with the Raja of Chandragiri

In the 18th century Rayalaseema, its adjoining areas and the hills abounded with wildlife and abundance of exotic birds. This made Rayalaseema a favorite hunting ground for the officers of the British East India Company, rajas, zamindars and the palegars. As was the custom, it was the turn of the Raja of Chandragiri to host the shikar and to make all the arrangements. The guest invitees were housed in the Chandragiri palace for the first two days, on the third day the entire lot of invitees and their subordinates which included their personal staff, bodyguards etc moved to tents set up on the instructions of the raja. Each tent was furnished with a bed, mattress, pillows, bedsheets and blankets, a washbasin, water, a writing table and a chair, a closed off lavatory with a English style commode, a bathing tub and lamps. Attendants would fan the distinguished guests throughout the night, provide water to drink and help in all other ways. For the purpose of dining a very large and colorful tent had been set up which had tables and chairs to seat at least 60 guests at any given point of time. An adjacent tent was set up for middle level and junior functionaries. Armed gorkhas and other guards were posted around the camps both at night and during the day to ensure wild animals and intruders were kept at bay.

The list of most honored guests who were invited to participate in the shikar by the Raja Shri Vijaya Rama Rao, Raja of Chandragiri, began with His Highness The Honorable Sir Charles Munroe G.C.S.I, G.B.E, G.C.I.E, Governor of Fort St.George, Madraspatnam, the Nawab of Arkot Nawab Mohammed Ali Khan Wallajah, the Raja of Venkatgiri Shri Harishcandra Naidu, the Raja of Bobbili Shri Devarakonda Vittal Dev Rao, the zamindar of Sompalyam Shri Govinda Krishna Rao, the zamindar of Rajanpalli Shri Jaganmohan Dev Rao, the palegar of Totlakonda Shri Thimmaraya VenkataRao, the palegar of Kovelakuntla Shri Veera Abbirami Reddy, the palegar of Kurnool Shri Narsimha Reddy, the palegar of Penukonda Shri Mal Kondiah, the palegar of Rayadurg Shri Gopala Krishna Reddy, the palegar of Kadiri Mirza Salahuddin along with his younger brother Mirza Ziauddin and a host of other smaller landlords.

The guest invitees also included functionaries of the British East India Company, senior and middle level military officers of the British East India Company, the only company in the world to have maintained a standing army of its own, to fight the wars waged by the company against the Afghans, the Sikhs, the Marathas, the Nawabs of Bengal and others from time to time over a period of approximately 250 years, until the rule of the company came to an end subsequent to the revolt of 1857. Thereafter India was brought directly under the control of The Queen of England and became an integral part of the British Empire, ruled by the Queen's chosen representative in India called the Viceroy. Last but not the least, the list of honored guests included the names of all members belonging to the family of the zamindar of Mahadevpalli, however only Shankar Dev Rao, Vikram Dev Rao, Bukka Dev Rao, Rudra Dev Rao and Yamini Devi could attend. The guests prior to the hunt or the shikar were initially housed in the palatial palace of the Raja of Chandragiri inside the Chandragiri fortress, which actually consists of two enclosures, the lower fort and the upper fort. The male guests were housed in the Raja Mahal or the King's palace and the female guests including family members and their female staff were housed in the Rani Mahal or the queen's palace. The guests met in the splendid durbar hall for discussions and friendly get togethers. It was in this very same durbar hall where the Shri Ranga Raya III the ruler of Chandragiri (whose illustrious lineage were once the rulers of Vijaynagar) signed the document granting the site in Madraspatnam on which the British East India Company built Fort St George in 1639 AD.

(At this juncture a pause in my narrative is a must to give the reader an idea as to how the Kingdom and the family of the Raja of Chandragiri came into existence. **The Golden Era of the Telugus was under the the Vijayanagara empire**. This empire consisted of several kingdoms and provinces. The governors under the direct control of the central government ruled the provinces and feudatory kings called "Nayakas" payed tribute to the king. The Vijayanagara Empire was plundered and its capital in Hampi was burnt after their army was defeated in the battle of Tallikota in 1565 AD, when the Muslim states consisting of Golconda, Bijapur, Ahmednagar and Bidar came together against the empire. Tirumala Deva Raya and his remaining forces fled to Vellore, Penukonda and Chandragiri where his successors ruled for another 81 years. Shri Ranga Raya lll, the last king whose lineage went back to the rulers of Vijaynagar following another debilitating battle with the Golkonda Sultanate, took refuge under his vassal Shivappa Nayaka of Ikkeri in Karnataka and died in 1678 AD. With this the rule of the Rayas came to an end. Thereafter various tributary kingdoms that flourished under the Vijayanagara Empire came under the control of the Sultans of Golconda and Bijapur. The Golconda and Bijapur Sultans employed Velama, Kamma and Reddy kings as the rulers of various kingdoms and ordered them to pay the tribute and collect revenue. Thus kingdoms/provinces, also known as Samsthanams or Zamindaris, came into existence. One of those Velama kingdoms which came into existence was the Kingdom of Chandragiri under an ancestor of the present ruler ie Sri Vijaya Rama Rao.

The Golconda sultanate, in due course of time came under the control of Mughal Dynasty in 1686 and became known as the Deccan Suba. The Mughals ruled the Deccan through their Governor Nizamul Ul Mulk

Asaf Jahi-l. With the decline of the Mughals, in the beginning the French had influence over Hyderabad ie over Golconda. Salabat Jung, who came to power after his father, realized that the French were losing ground to British/English forces and so he realigned himself with the English ie the British East India Company. However, in 1761, the East India Company helped Nizam Ali Khan to depose his brother Salabat Jung and occupy the Deccan Suba.The East India Company took the Andhra regions for lease from Nizam Ali. Later, according to the accords of 1768 and 1779 the Andhra regions came under the complete control of the East India Company including Rayalseema "which came to be known as the territory ceded by the Nizam of Hyderabad to the British East India Company or simply as the ceded territory", while the Telagana states remained under the Nizam. In 1802, the British government under a Permanent Revenue Settlement agreement restored the ruling powers and rights of the kings of the Andhra regions. During this time, rich and influential people were able to become rulers "Zamindars" to the city-states "Zamindaris". In the beginning, the British allowed old kingdoms to have armies with the condition that they would support the British Empire during the war. However this right to have and maintain an army was abolished later and kings were reduced to the level of Zamindars).

The maharajas, the rajas and the zamindars were instrumental in forging the regal hunt and lavishly expressed hospitality to various European and British dignitaries by providing them shikar in their preserves in the princely states as well as feasts and amusement in the form of dancing girls in their palaces. The bond between the shikaris ie hunters and the maharajas, rajas and zamindars represented an unusual relationship between the higher and the lower order because of the unpretentiousness of the royals and their oneness with other shikaris while hunting in the jungle.

Historical Perspective of the "hunt" during the Mughal period from the 16th century onwards: The Mughals were foreign Muslim rulers and they hunted animals by the hundreds. The Mughals hunted by forming a "hunting circle" which was a man made enclosure with men standing in a circle to encompass the wild game and then shoot it with bows and arrows on horseback while using a sword to kill the animal. The Mughals like the British wrote down the names of all the animals and birds that they hunted. These accounts were very descriptive and they took pains to record the colour of different varieties of deer, the activities of monkeys, the beauty of peacocks etc. Pretty birds and hunting scenes were sought after and the Mughal Emperors ordered their artists to capture this beauty. On the other hand the British, during the British Raj in India did not commission artists to create the picturesque scenes, preferring to sketch it themselves. The Mughals used hunting cheetahs, rather than shikaris to accompany them on their hunting expeditions. Control over wild game was essential for the Mughals as they asserted authority over their native subjects. They also maintained enclosed hunting grounds called the "qamarga" where corporal punishment was given by trampling a prisoner under the feet of an elephant as punishment for his crime.

On the first day of the hunt the Raja of Chandragiri formed a human ring of beaters, who drove deer and other animals into a ring, which made it easy for the invitees to kill. The hunt was masterminded by a group of local hunters called 'shikharis', which was headed by a 'mir shikaran' or the headshikari. They tracked the animal on foot with the help of a large retinue of beaters, while the Governor, the Kings, Zamindars and Palegars rode on horse or elephant back. When found, the animal would be forced out of its cover by 'beaters' with drums, sticks and lathis. When the animal was cornered, the king and some of his guests would shoot the animal. More often than not, royalty accorded the king the privilege of firing the first bullet. In this case the privilege was accorded to Sir Charles Munroe. On subsequent days of the hunt or shikar, the killing fields was not restricted to land alone in Rayalaseema and its surrounding areas, the shikar went on in marshes, lakes and rivers, barges and boats were used to carry out hunting, fishing and fowling with the help of decoys, nets and guns. The culling of dangerous game such as tigers was testament to the attributes of daring and courage, which were sought by the British, the kings, the zamindars and the palegars alike. It made men proficient in the art of stalking, while ensuring that they remained fit. Keeping with the guileful ways of regency, hunting was a way to mask invasions upon unsuspecting kingdoms. Thus the techniques employed, demanded levels of precision, planning and discipline akin to those used in the army. The 'qamargarh' or crescent shaped formation or the 'nihilam' and 'tashqawal', which were ring-shaped, fenced hunts were commonly employed techniques ie techniques used by the Mughals. The game would be driven into these fenced portions which were lined with fluttering strips of cloth that frightened the animals into remaining within the enclosure, after which the slaying would begin.

As far as His Highness the Honorable Sir Charles Munroe, Governor of Fort St.George was concerned, he took full advantage of the unrestrained shikar and strengthened the ties of the British East India Company with the rajas, zamindars and the palegars.

Since the King of Chandragiri had organized the extravaganza, almost every member of the local populace was involved in the royal beat. The Royal hunt showcased the British and the Indian triumph over Indian wildlife as the grandness of the hunt was evident in its numbers. A large number of the local population was engaged as beaters whose job was to beat the foliage back and reveal the hidden animals and as far as the guests were concerned hunting was restricted to pulling the trigger. The hunt also displayed a sheer sense of excess as a large number of animals were killed.

Grand, colorful tents were ptiched or set up close to the hunting destinations. The tent material, beds, bedding etc was brought by dozens of bullock carts, with coolies, kansamas ie cooks and beaters along with "natch" girls ie dancing girls, concubines and slave girls. These girls provided entertainment after a hard day's hunt and many nights of sexual cavorting under a moon or a star lit sky. The bullock carts also carried a wide variety of weapons such as bows and arrows, nets, swords, daggers, matchlocks and flintlocks along with hunting dogs, cheetahs, hawks and falcons.

18th century dog breeds used by the zamindars in Rayalaseema to track down their opponents and to hunt wild animals:

Chippiparai hound, one of the many hound breeds, bred by royal families in Chippiparai near Madurai, present day Tamil Nadu, was primarily used for hunting boar, deer and hare.

The Rampur Greyhound, a native to the Rampur region in Northern India that lies between Delhi and Bareilly was a preferred breed by Maharajas to hunt big game and protect against fierce animals like lions, tigers, leopards and panthers. The Rampur Hound was known for its endurance as it was built to cover large distances at great speed.

Another hound from South India, the Kombai (Combai) was bred to hunt boar, bison and deer as early as the 9th Century. In comparison with the Rajapalayam, the Kombai has a tan coat with usually a black muzzle. The jaws are wider and much stronger as well.

The Kanni is a rare indigenous breed from South India. They are closely related to the Chippiparai and are said to be descendants of the Saluki. These breeds were built to hunt deer as they are very agile and light on their feet. Usually a silent dog, they are great as guards of their owners and easy to train. However, they act independent when on a hunt as is their disposition.

Mandai in Tamil language means head. Mandai dogs have big heads and are very ferocious. They are assigned guard duty by land owners to ward off intruders.

The royal hunt was a way to exert dominion over nature. Therefore, cheetahs and lynx were tamed and sent after antelopes, while smaller game such as partridge, fowl, hare and other creatures were pinned down as part of the 'art' of falconry. In the former, cheetahs were either trapped in the wild or bred and trained to hunt. The lithe animals were hooded until they were within adequate distance of the king's or the zamindar's quarry, after which they were unmasked and set after their prey. As soon the hapless game was brought down, the king, zamindar or his attendants would slay the creature. As a reward, the cheetah would be treated to a part of the animal's hindquarters.

Falconry

Falconry was especially popular during the 18th century. While the eagle's courage and strength were appreciated, fortunately or unfortunately for the falcon, its speed and agility won it favor. Most beloved among the latter were 'goshawks' and 'sakers'. Usually, one or two of these birds would be taken to the hunting grounds. The king, the zamindar and his attendants would stalk the quarry for a while. At a carefully calculated moment, the falconer would release the birds from their hooded perch to chase the quarry. They would then attack the head or nape of the quarry and injure it after which, a 'shikari' would administer the final deathblow to the animal. Many a time, falcons would hunt in tandem with cheetahs and dogs. The use of decoys to distract and hunt antelope as well as waterfowl was also popular. Other animals that were killed, included nilgai, gazelle, leopards and tigers as well as birds such as francolins, cranes, ibises etc.

Tiger Hunt

Tiger hunting however remained a matter of pride, the tiger, which inspired awe and fear in man, was an object to be overcome by way of the royal hunt. The tiger would be surrounded by a line of elephants to prevent it from escaping and then it became an easy target which did not require much physical prowess from the shooter.

The reasons for killing the tiger were many. It was regarded a “scourge” that preyed on man and beast and the subcontinent was expected to be obliged to her conquerors for their efforts in eradicating this creature. The two most favoured methods of hunting a tiger were either on a beat or “buttue” (as the French called it) or by using bait. In the first method, a trained tracker called a 'shikari' would comb the jungles for any sign of the animal. Once the animal was found, the hunter would head to the forest on elephant or horseback. The hunting party that consisted of beaters and troopers would set out on foot. With the help of drums, firecrackers and loud clanging noises, they would send the game scurrying in the direction of the hunters. When the tiger was well within range of the hunter's gun, it was quickly dispatched. Many hunters speak delightedly of the joy of seeing the confused animal as they sat perched on their elephants. In the second method, a calf or a goat was often tied to a spot, which was known to be frequented by tigers while a shikari kept watch. A 'machan' or a wooden platform was constructed in the trunk of a nearby tree, which was the hunter's perch. After sundown, the hunter kept watch from the machan and should the tiger have acquired a taste for the meat of domestic cattle, its death was almost certain. Sometimes, the hunter arrived until after a kill was made and would shoot as the tiger fed on the carcass. The quarry was then measured and skinned or stuffed. Many a time, the flesh was given to local villagers and tribesman as a token for their effort in the hunt. Tigers were also tracked on foot but only skilled, accomplished hunters resorted to this method. In India, the beat was the method that was used whereas hunters in the southern regions preferred to track it on foot. This method was also employed to kill other elusive carnivores like leopards, and cheetahs. Meanwhile, guns continued to be trained on most wild animals and birds. Blackbuck, nilgai, leopards, deer, barasingha, wild buffaloes, elephants, sloth bears etc. were all hunted, some as trophies while others for meat. Another popular sport was pig-sticking, wherein men on horseback would employ the beat and spear wild boars that emerged from the forest cover.

Pig Sticking

Pig sticking even had its own Super Bowl – the Kadir Cup – its own toast – "To the Boar!" and its own songs, most probably sung after several toasts. A number of artists illustrated the sport for magazines and prints, most notably Charles Johnson Payne (1884-1967), who signed his sketches "Snaffles.". Its essence was described by Major General J.G. Elliott in his Field Sports in India 1800-1947:

"Armed with a nine-foot lance, the pig-sticker rode a galloping horse in pursuit of wild boar which had been flushed out of the bush by beaters. The aim was to stick the boar immediately behind the shoulder, so that the spear would pass through the lungs and out of the breast." The sporting aspect came from the marked reluctance of the boar to cooperate. The boars of India grew upto five feet in length and three feet at the shoulder, Elliott wrote of one bad boy who measured 44 inches at the shoulder and weighed more than 400 pounds. Such boars ran as fast as a horse, could make a 90-degree turn at a full gallop, a practice known as "jinking", and came armed with curved tusks up to 9 inches long, sharp teeth and a profoundly irritable disposition. When unable to outrun its pursuer, the boar turned and charged. In the middle was the horse, which could be cut, even killed, by the boar's tusks and once speared, boars were known to struggle upwards on the lance to get to the wide-eyed man at the end. Leaving the boar aside, the pursuit in itself was dangerous. Elliott notes, "The horse had to be able to remain upright when galloping full tilt through thick grass six to nine feet high, over ground as hard as rock, seamed with large and small nullahs [steep, narrow watercourses, usually dry] and the occasional sunken buffalo wallow. Old, disused wells, completely overgrown by long grass, were a constant hazard.

When a hunt was organized, every thing went into a tizzy. Trackers were sent into forests to ensure the abundance of game, the higher the rank of the official, the greater were the demands to be met. It was a matter of prestige for a district to be able to produce fine quarry.

On the one hand, the razing of forests and the killing of animals was an extension of the British penchant for order and discipline in place of all, that was unruly and wild. On the other hand, it was a front to keep a check on the administration of the provinces. The beat consisted primarily of locals that would track the animal and deliver it to the hunter. Etiquette demanded that the region's local officers be invited on the hunt thus giving the administration a chance to observe and study the region's terrain and topography while aiding the development of the field of natural history. Infact, most naturalists and hunters were keen marksmen who regularly took to hunting and study of their quarry. The British officers often complained that native shikaris did not follow the hunting etiquette of keeping quiet while stalking game. These native shikaris sometimes talked to the sahibs while waiting for game, prayed for the kill, adjusted their pugrees (headgear) or beat off flies. This was a major problem for British officers who preferred silence so that the kill could be quickly achieved. The death of an animal marked the masculine prowess of the shooter and also the clamor in the forest where coolies would be sent to drag the body of the animal back to the village in order to have it skinned and the meat distributed along with a nice trophy.The trophy was the ultimate prize of a hunt. Hunters chose which animals to shoot on the basis of whether or not they would serve as good trophies, as trophies were regarded as symbols of masculine identity.

The Ultimate Prize Trophy

Prized skins of tigers along with other trophies which included the heads of leopards, black panthers, gaurs (wild bison), wild boar and a variety of deer, adorned the walls of the bungalows where the governor and his officers stayed, the walls of palaces in which the rajas stayed and the walls of the mansions in which the zamindars lived. From among the trophies, the tiger was the ultimate prize trophy mainly because of the animal's reputation as a ferocious beast. The records of hunting expeditions were preserved through the transformation of select tiger remains, like skins and the head into a trophy. Furthermore it was necessary to tabulate the lengths and the widths of the animals that were killed.

As part of the entertainment for the honored guests highly skilled dancers entertained the guests as mentioned. These dancers were valued for their intelligence as well as their dancing skills and were at least partially educated. As a form of employment they offered sexual services and were often seen wearing costly jewellery. They had a reputation for connecting sex with music and dance. The name "nauch" comes from Prakrit "nacha" meaning dance. Most natch girls were trained to dance as children, some were slaves and others had been sold by their parents. Every Hindu temple of any importance processed a troupe of natch girls, some acted as priestesses, married in childhood to the idols and obligated by the imposed terms of their vocation to prostitute themselves to men of every caste. Others acted as mistresses to temple priests. However such prostitution was not looked down upon in those days and even distinguished families were proud to have daughters dedicated to the temple's service. For the Britishers and westerners, the natch girls were the embodiment of sexuality, highly erotic seductresses who had the ability to charm all males. Indeed in the 18th century, travellers frequently potrayed India as a hotbed of vice and of prostitutes. Their apparent ability to bedazzle men, with rings on their fingers and bells on their anklets, they stomped and gyrated their way into the hearts of the onlookers. The strange and intoxicating effct the natch girls had over men bred in England who were admired and respected by their country men cannot be accounted for. The only explanation, it seemed was that the natch girls held some kind of mystical spell over men. The influence of the natch girls was comparable to an intoxicating drug. The natch girls had a mesmeric effect on men with their music and dance which drew the enchanted lovers to them. There was a strong belief that the dancing girls practised tantric sex and the crux of this ritual lay in its connection with the magically induced ecstasies of sexual orgasm. Tantric sex was a journey, to explore pleasure for pleasure's sake and to surrender into an ocean of erotic unknown mystery, a journey from which those who undertook it, rarely if ever returned. Sexual energy which passed between the individuals involved in sex with the natch girls, had a strange, binding as well as a blinding effect which made the male recipient ie male paramour, come back time and again, even if in the process of catering to the demands of the natch girls for costly gifts, many a male recipient ie male paramour was driven into poverty, penury, alcohol addiction and drug abuse. There are innumerable examples of rajas, nawabs and zamindars who after having lost their property and their status in society while catering to the demands of the natch girls, eventually came to work for or to borrow money for their own livelihood from the very same natch girls whom they once patronised.

The Governor and his entourage were so enamored of these natch girls that they found the songs that the girls sang very enticing inspite of the fact that the songs were highly objectionable and lewd. The governor, the rajas and the zamindars gave them precious jewellery and squandered large sums of money on them. The wives of the invitees who had accompanied their husbands complained that their husbands had forsaken them at night for these natch girls. In large cities like Madras, the general opinion was that a man is not worth his position if he does not patronize a natch girl ie a dancing girl.

Bukka had brought six of his most beautiful natch girls for the event. When Pampa, Shona, Putli, Komala, Shamma and Shabnum danced with gay abandon, the effect was spellbinding on the Governor and the other guests. Bukka plied the dignitaries with copious amounts of port, a variety of wines, cordials and brandies along with hookahs to smoke. He ensured the very best quality of claret was served to the Governor, the Nawab of Arcot and the Rajas.

On this occasion it was the turn of Pampa and Shona to dance. Pampa and Shona wore identical maroon Kanjivaram silk sarees with a gold border.They lined their large and beautiful eyes with kajal or khol, their maids plaited their thick, black, long and lustrous hair, adorning it with fresh jasmine flowers. The maids first applied turmeric and then a thin delicate pattern of red alta colour ie a red coloured dye, to their feet. Both of them selected similar gold bangles, similar gold earings studded with precious stones and diamonds. They had received a lot of jewellery from Bukka and from other paramours. They wore gold jewellery studded with emeralds, rubies, sapphires and diamonds on their forehead, ears, neck, waist, forearms and wrists apart from beautifully designed emerald, ruby, sapphire and diamond studded rings on their fingers, gold anklets and gold toe rings. They used a part of their saree to cover their heads and a part of their face while making a dazzling entrance on the stage, offered their salaams to the distinguished guests, they avoided any eye contact and drew their saree aside just before dancing. They could dance with the grace of a deer or the swiftness of an eagle, all of which called for several hours of strenuous training and practice. The audience went into raptures, Sir Charles could not take his ravenous eyes off Pampa to whom he had taken a fancy, she knew that look all too well, she had made up her mind that she was not going to bed with him. As the duo started to dance there was a lot of commotion and catcalls from the rear of the tent, this did not distract the dancers, as they gyrated and continued with their performance. Large sums of money in the form of gold and silver coins were thrown on the stage for them to collect. Sometimes on an indication from Bukka one of the dancers would break away from the dance and approach Sir Charles who would pat her on her buttocks and give her a bagfull of silver coins. Sometimes he would try and hold one of them with a look of drunken desire in his eyes. He treated them as concubines, whores selling sex and this was evident from the way he asked them to sit on his lap while running his hand over their body. Both Pampa and Shona had come a long way from the days when they sold themselves and their services. Now they had enough wealth to be discerning with regard to who they wished to entertain and who it was beneath their dignity to entertain. The tables had turned, they ie the concubines were calling the shots, they no longer wanted to be treated as low class natch girls and this made them reject many a poorer customer. Both of them had seen performances in the big cities and had gone through very ugly days, many days of starvation and it was not without reason that Sir Charles's behaviour was beginning to irritate them. After all, they were high class natch girls but the firangi was continuing to treat them as nothing more than low class whores. However they were too adept at the game of concealment to wear their feelings on their shoulders, humoring the "white firangi" was the very reason behind the shikar, the lavish arrangements, the starry nights with slave girls and the natch girls. (The natch girls also felt that the very reason for the proliferation of brothels was because of the British East India company which maintained an army and provided the services of native women exclusively to their "English" soldiers as a welfare measure. They also had good reasons to despise the white firangi, because it was the policy of the British East India Company to dump cheap factory made cloth and other items in the Indian markets. As a result many local artisans lost their source of livelihood, their only source of earning and as a result their womenfolk were driven into destitution and ultimately prostitution. There was also a genuine fear in their minds that if the "white firangi" took too much of a liking to them and asked for them to be sent back with him, it would pose a very big problem, because refusing outright could be construed as an act of defiance, an insult which would have bad consequences. On the other hand they had come to love and respect Bukka for his kindness and generosity, he was a benevolent patron as far as they were concerned in his dealings with them. They did not want to put him or his father, the zamindar in an awkward position. Under the circumstances when there was a brief interlude, Pampa informed Bukka about their apprehension. He agreed that there was a very grave possibility that Sir Charles could ask them to accompany him back to Madras. Bukka understood the gravity of the situation and casually introduced Sir Charles to smoking a hookah, but this hookah was laced with charas or ganja ie marijuana, the fumes had an intoxicating effect and Sir Charleas Munroe, the Governor of Fort St George, Madras fell asleep and awoke the next morning without any memory of the natch girls with whom he was infatuated the previous night. Fortunately it was also the day on which Sir Charles Munroe had to go back to Madras where he was scheduled to receive two senior directors of the British East India Company accompanied by their wives. Both the directors were his immediate superiors, they were arriving by ship on a visit to India and to take stock of the company's plans.

In four weeks of the hunting a dozen tigers, seven leopards, nine bears, six gaur or bison, over two dozen wild boars and over three dozen deer like the black buck, sambar, cheetal and in addition any number of wild pheasants, ducks, partridges and other exotic birds were hunted down and killed. The animals were skinned and the pelt was put out to dry, the flesh was cooked for the dignitaries in a variety of ways. The Royal penchant for fine dining was also part of the inspiration behind the royal hunt. The typical menu included at least 30-40 dishes with a wide range of meats, many of which came from wild, exotic creatures that roamed the hunting grounds. A large number of cooks, coolies and servants were required for skinning and cooking the meat from the game that was shot. Hunting provided the governor, rajas, zamindars and the palegars a variety of dishes. The guests enjoyed eating a variety of kababs such as the mouth watering tunde kabab, mutton (boneless) pasanda kabab, sheek kabab (which has its origin in Greece), shammi kabab (originally from "Sham" ie an Arabic word for Syria), kakori kabab (named after Kakori, a place about 12 kms from Lucknow), galouti Kabab (meant to literally melt in the mouth, easy to digest), tootak kabab (made from mutton kheema and suji baked together) and the shikampur kabab. Apart from kababs other dishes such as haleem, dum-pukht-biryani, nur-mahal-biryani, Hyderabadi-kacchi-biryani, mussalam mutton, mussalam fish, mussalam bater was cooked and served. To cater to the taste ie zaika, mussalam bakra-ka-rand, mussalam teetar in gravy and pattar-ka-gosh (mutton cooked on a heated granite stone slab) was cooked by experienced cooks or khansamas. Mutton kurma, mutton curry with a variety of vegetable dishes and roomali roti, the famous Nizam Kulcha was on the daily menu. Sweets included from among others the shahi tookda, phirni, kali-gajar-ka-halwa, double-ka-meetai and kubani-ka-meetai. The food was cooked in copper vessels with kalai ie tin coating, this was meant to give "kushta" ie virility. Great care was taken to ensure that the richness ie the "razaayiyat", of food was balanced by the zaika ie taste and "kushta". The food was meant to give strength to the hunters to hunt through out the day as well as to cope with the nocturnal demands of concubines, slaves and natch girls. Only freshly cooked food was served, out of season vegetable dishes were avoided, "be-wakt-ke-tarkari-nahi-khaya-jata" ie out of season vegetable dishes were not cooked nor were they eaten. The delicacies also included "khad-kargosh (rabbit cooked in a pit with coal fire).

After the shikar the guests were given costly gold gifts as a mark of respect. Before they left the Royal palace at Chandragiri, Sir Charles Munro was presented a diamond necklace as a mark of respect in keeping with his position and the power he wielded.

Painting: Boyakonda Gangamma

Chapter 9

The First Pilgrimage

A pilgrimage to Vontimetta & a visit to Madhavaram

On the insistance of Yamini Devi the whole family with the exception of Shankar Dev Rao, Bukka and Rudra (who stayed back ostensibly to attend to some important pending work, but in reality the reason for staying back was to engage in philandering) undertook a pilgrimage to the famous Kodandarama temple in Vontimetta. A convoy of 24 bullock carts was used to transport 6 family members including relatives and 18 attendants including six cooks, six female and six male helpers along with clothes, food items, mattresses with bedsheets to sleep on, bronze or khanshu cooking utensils and massive copper urns to carry fresh water. The bullock carts also carried tent material to put up four tents in an array of colors for family members and female helpers to sleep at night. The rest of the male members including the guards had to sleep in the open, under a star lit sky.

The bullock carts were beautifully painted with floral patterns, the horns of the bulls were also colored in red, blue, green and yellow colors and each bull had a brass bell around its neck. The net effect was that the chiming of the bells as the bullocks moved could be heard for quite some distance. In addition 16 well armed bodyguards accompanied the convoy on horseback along with Vikram and Surya who rode along on horseback.

The trip to Vontimetta took a couple of days, travelling at night was avoided not only because of the harsh terrain but also because of armed gangs of robbers. (Armed robbers that roamed the vast plains of Rayalaseema were a menace and this ensured that despite the heat most people preferred to travel by day and rest in a well fortified temple or a village at night). At night neem oil lamps were lit to provide sufficient lighting in addition to the light coming from the bonfire around which the family members sat (nights in the vast open stretches of Rayalaseema is known to be very cold and chilly especially when the wind picks up speed) under a star filled sky singing songs or telling stories, while their cooks prepared jowar rotis, rice, dhal and vegetable curries. Lakshmi Devi, her mother Maheshwari Devi and Bukka's wife Parvathi Devi were in their element. They outdid the rest in singing anthyakshari songs. The staff members accompanying the family members ate raagi mudda or raagi sankati prepared with finger millets (this food was not easy to digest but it gave them strength and stamina) along with the excess rotis and vegetables.

According to legend, the temple at Vontimitta was built by Vontudu and Mittudu, two robbers turned devotees of Lord Rama. According to history the temple was built by the Chola Kings and further expanded by the Vijaynagara kings. The temple itself is known for its architectural elegance, having 3 ornate gopurams, one facing east which is the entrance to the temple and the other two facing north and south. The Mandapam or the Rangmantapam, essentially an open air theatre of sorts with 32 exquisitely sculptured pillars. The sculptures of Lord Rama and Laxmana are also seen in this mandapa, Lord Rama is depicted with a bow in his right hand and an arrow in his left hand, hence the name Kodanda Rama, on the other hand Lakshmana is depicted in the tribhanga position with his right hand free, while holding a bow in his left hand. The sanctum sanctorum has the statue of Lord Rama, Sita and Lakshmana carved out of a single block of stone. The saint poet Annamacharya is said to have visited the temple, composed and sung songs in praise of Lord Rama. Jean Baptite Tavernier, the French traveller and historian, visited the temple in 1652 AD.

That night Yamini Devi decided that they would spend the night within the walls of the temple, it was much safer. At night burning brands of wood with the tip coated in oil was used to light up the vast space around the main temple. The sanctum sanctorum was closed after the last pooja of the day. This pooja was done at 8 0'clock at night. Spending one night inside the temple lit by burning brands of wood and lamp light was a strangely ethereal and fulfilling experience. They cooked and ate inside the temple walls and the family members slept on mattresses with bed sheets spread on them placed on the floor within the stone pillared halls of the temple.

The next day early in the morning, after the morning pooja in the temple Lakshmi Devi, the grand daughter of the zamindar insisted that they must visit the ancient village of Madhavaram, made famous because of the exquisite sarees woven by skilled weavers in that village and in the surrounding villages and then the temple of Lord Balaji on Tirumala, spend at least two days in the temple and then go to Vadamalpet on the way back after spending some time in the family mango orchard in Vadamalpet for a few days. Since Lakshmi Devi's marriage was in the offing and after marriage it would not be possible for her to regularly join or take part in family functions in Mahadevpalli, Yamini Devi readily agreed (Yamini Devi was very fond of her grand daughter Lakshmi Devi) and the convoy turned towards Madhavaram. (Madhavaram sarees came from villages or gramas nestled in between the Penna River and majestic hills, the sarees were made in a simple and soothing fashion by very skilled weavers from the Togata community. These sarees or cheeras are a must in all weddings that take place in Rayalaseema. A host of colors ranging from pink, pale blue, red and black were used in the sarees to create patterns that were usually alternating squares or floral designs. The sarees were regular or they had a pattu ie a border, the "Modugu puvvu" was used to give a traditional reddish color to the border).

18th century Woman in Saree

On seeing a number of sarees displayed by the villagers, Lakshmi Devi exclaimed "they are beautiful, nanamma I want to buy at least 12 of them", Yamini Devi replied "take what you like", Parvathi and Maheshwari who were silent could not contain themselves any longer and joined the milieu in selecting sarees for themselves and for others in the group. Even the staff and the servants bought a few sarees of the cheaper kind for their womenfolk. Maheshwari picked up a saree with a peacock hue and asked "how does this saree look on me?" Parvathi replied "akka it suits you, you look beautiful", Lakshmi Devi interrupted to say "what about this maroon saree, it has a unique border", Yamini Devi said "it will look good on you." The conversation on the colour, the tone, the shade, the hue, the texture and the feel, which saree to buy, the suitable combination of sarees which suited a particular person went on for a while until everyone had picked up what they wanted, then Yamini Devi paid for the whole lot and it was time to go to the temple of Lord Balaji onTirumala.

The journey from Madhavaram to Tirumala took two full days. Going up the Tirumala or the hill on which the temple of Lord Balaji is located was on foot, since there was no road leading up to the hill. The menfolk walked on narrow winding mountain pathways to the temple located on top of the hill. The women were carried in beautiful, colored palanquins, each palanquin was lifted by a minimum of four or five sturdy men. A large number of sturdy villagers residing close to the foothills of the Tirumala Hills were hired by Vikram Dev Rao not only to carry the palanquins but also to carry the other material such as mattresses to sleep on, tent material, food, water in very large copper urns etc which was earlier on carried by bullock carts.

Religious perspective: Tirumala Dhruva Bera is the name given to the idol of Lord Venkateswara in the Tirumala Venkateswara Temple, Andhra Pradesh. Dhruva Bera is the official terminology used for the main deity of a temple, with the exact translation being the immobile image and as the name suggests, the idol is stationary and other idols are used for pujas, sevas that requires the deity's presence outside the garbha griham (sanctum sanctorum). Other terms used for Dhruva Bera include Moolavar or Moola Virat (Main Deity), Achala (Main).

Tirumala Dhruva Bera is considered to be Swayambhu ie self-manifested and not created by humanbeings. According to Sri Venkatachala Mahatyam, Lord Venkateswara came to reside in this sacred spot to provide blessings to devotees in the Kali Yuga. The idol does not conform to the agamas (rules) for making a deity, thus furthering the belief that the temple's idol is Swayambhu.

The dhruva bera stands approximately ten feet tall and stands on a platform of about 18 inches. The platform follows a simple lotus design and the detail of any inscription on the platform is unknown to anyone except the temple's archakas (priests). The platform is usually covered in tulsi leaves except on Thursday afternoon and during Friday abhishekam.

The face of the idol has exquisite features, with the nose neither flat nor prominent. The eyes are prominent and have the outline of 'namam' though it is not projected out of the idol. The eyes are partially covered with the namam made of pachakarpuram (raw camphor). The size, shape and details of the namam are governed by strict rules laid by the Vaikhanasa agamam. The idol has a self manifested crown up to the forehead and jatajuta (curly hair) resting on the shoulder. The chest is estimated to be between 36 to 40 inches in width and the waist would be between 24 to 27 inches, though there has never been a formal measurement of these statistics. Since the upper body is bare, features of the chest are prominently seen with the main feature being the image of a sitting Sridevi carved on the right side of the chest. The image of Lakshmi is integral to the idol. The idol has 4 arms. The upper arms are in the position to hold his weapons, though the Chakram and Conch are not integral to the idol. The removable Sudarshana chakram is placed on the upper right arm while the Panchajanya – Vishnu's conch is placed on the upper left arm. The lower right arm is in the Varada Hasta pose – palms facing outward towards the onlooker to signal boon giving nature of the Lord. The lower left arm is in the Katyavalambita pose – palm facing the lord with the thumb nearly parallel to the waist. The idol is seen with a dhoti worn waist downwards. Both the knees are slightly bent forward to indicate that the Lord is willing to come to the devotee's rescue. The shoulder of the Lord has marks resembling scars made by constant wearing of a bow and a pack of arrows though the idol is not in the Tribhanga pose (unlike the Tirumala Rama Idol).

After spending more than three nights and two days in Tirumala and after doing pooja to Lord Venkateshwara atleast thrice a day, after putting a very large sum of money in the form of gold and silver coins in the hundi and after feeding over a thousand devotees on both days, it was decided to come down the Tirumala hills and go to the zamindar's family owned mango orchard in Vadamalpet which was spread over several hundred acres of land with an ancient but spacious house or bungalow in the middle where all the family members and their staff settled down to stay for about a week. A large number of Banganapalli, Badami, Neelam, Raspuri, Malgoa and Totapuri mango trees grew in different sections of the vast orchard. The orchard was inhabited by a large number of deer, wild boar, leopards and a variety of birds not to mention the fish that grew in a very large, natural pond in front of bungalow. The water from the pond was very clean and was used for cooking, washing clothes, bathing and for all domestic work. However, great care was taken to ensure that the water remained pure by diverting all dirty water to a system of drains away from the pond. The mango trees were irrigated through a system of small canals that criscrossed the orchard, water for irrigation was drawn from a massive manmade reservoir which lay to the north of the orchard at a distance of about 3 kms. The family and staff members busied themselves with various activities including cooking, playing games, singing, enjoying the beauty of nature, the fauna and the flora. In general the idea was to spend time together, to strengthen family ties, to take time out to talk to other family members and the staff, most of whom were treated as part of the family, this fostered a sense of wellbeing and closeness.

Food was an elaborate affair which involved cooking a large number of dishes which is associated with the people of Rayalaseema. Ragi Sangati with chicken curry, dumplings made with fermented urad dal ie black gram and rice batter or Gunta punugulu made from left over idli or dosa batter that was poured into a special pan that had hollow spaces and cooked, was the staple food for the staff. Family members also joined in, on a few days. Uggani and Bajji along with Vada made of alasanda or black eyed peas were eaten as a snack. At times this alasanda vada was dipped in chicken gravy or potato kurma ie potato stew and eaten. Breakfast consisted of a variety of Karam Dosas such as the erra karam dosa ie dosa with red chilli powder, the pachi karam dosa ie dosa with raw green chilli chutney, the mixed karam dosa. The erra karam dosa was eaten with chutney made by grinding red chillies, garlic, onion and mustard seeds along with pappu podi ie roasted and ground gram flour. The pachi karam dosa was eaten with chutney made of green chillies, onions, and coriander. The mixed karam dosa was eaten with both the chutneys. The Karam Dosa was considered to be one of the hottest and spiciest preparations. For lunch there was Mutton or chicken Biryani prepared in earthenware pots alongwith Natu Kodi Pulusu, Sweet and Sour Pachi ie raw Pulusu made with tamarind juice which makes it refreshing and sour along with jaggery that contributes sweetness followed by eating Annam ie rice with chicken curry, Appadam, Rasam and Perugu ie curd. The curry leaves, roasted chillies, spices and coriander gave Rayalaseema food its unique flavour and freshness. The meal was concluded with sweets such as Bhakshyalu, made from chana dal stuffed with a mix of coconut and jaggery and Bobbatlu with a filling called purnam.

In Vadamalpet Vikram Dev Rao arranged for a spectacular show of Vajra Mushti. Two of the best pairs of wrestlers were brought from the Princely state of Mysore for the performance. The meaning of Vajra Mushti is "thunderbolt fist" Vajra Mushti is an ancient Indian martial art considered a unique martial art that combines wrestling, grappling and striking techniques into one fluid system. This martial art is characterized by grappling and striking attacks aimed at vital pressure points. It also incorporates the use of small metal weapons, similar to western brass knuckles. In Vajra Mushti, knuckledusters made of animal horns are used as a weapon held in the right hand. The goal is to immobilize the opponent's hand holding the knuckle duster. Vajra Mushti is a no holds barred martial art. A fight is considered over, when one immobilizes the opponent's knuckleduster. Vajra Mushti dates back to the 5th century AD. The name is derived from Vajra, a religious symbol in both Hinduism and Buddhism meaning thunderbolt and Mushti, meaning closed fist. Training in Vajra Mushti was very intensive. In Vajra Mushti students were taught a variety of striking techniques similar to kung fu, boxing, karate and grappling techniques similar to jujitsu and vale tudo.

Historical perspective of Vajra Mushti: In the 18th century, Vajra Mushti Kalaga wrestling came alive during Vijayadashami celebrations in Mysore.

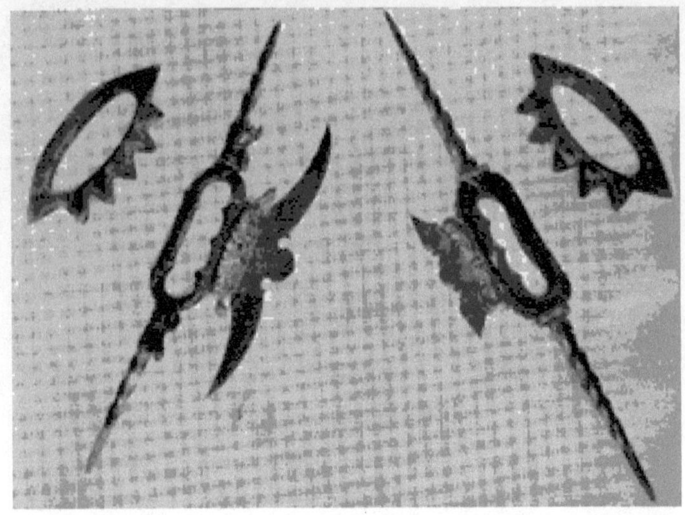

Here are some examples of the various Vajramushtis, the two smaller weapons were used for the sporting events, whilst the larger ones, complete with spiked ends, were used in warfare.

The event was held at Karikallu Thotti in front of the Kalyana Mantap of the Mysore Palace and was organised with all its traditional fervour and as per the age old customs. The ritual heralded the Dasara procession. The tradition has it that when two Jattis ie wrestlers, wearing the Vajra, wrestle and the moment the blood is drawn from the head of one of the wrestlers, it signals the start of the Dasara procession. Later on that day, Wrestlers, with shaved heads and wearing knuckledusters with spikes, engaged their respective combatants in the duel. The knuckledusters, made of metal and ivory, are in the possession of the royal family. They are offered a puja before they are given to the wrestlers. The wrestlers, while evading the assault with one arm, try to heave blows on the opponent's shaven head with the other hand bearing the knuckleduster. The duel ends with the draw of first blood from one of the wrestlers.

On the day of the match, the combatants' heads are shaved clean, except for a small tuft of hair on the crown of the head. Several Neem leaves are tied to this tuft of hair as a good luck omen. The wrestler's body is then rubbed down with red ochre, which is supposedly meant to keep the body cool during the fight. Before leaving their family Akhada for the match, both fighters pray to their family Goddess, Limbaja. For this worship, a square altar is temporarly constructed in the middle of the wrestling pit, upon which a branch of the Neem tree is planted. To the east of this altar, a small platform is placed, upon which, the weapons of the wrestlers are placed. After prayers and rituals are completed, the fighter is given the Vajramushti, which is tied to his right hand. Upon leaving their family's place of training, the wrestlers make their way to the public arena, where they enter in a zig- zag, jumping fashion.The object of the match was to bring the other fighter to the point of submission, either by showering blows to the head or a locking up of the Vajramushti-wielding arm. It is a limited-rules engagement, where knees, kicks and strikes are all legal techniques to be used in conjunction with grappling techniques. Both fighters receive payment after the match, the winner received double the amount of his defeated opponent. If the match was a draw and neither fighter was subdued by the other fighter, then the prize was shared.

The return journey was a quiet affair except for a short engagement with a gang of robbers who mistook the convoy for a convoy of wealthy merchants. They soon realized that this was a different crowd altogether, the bodyguards put the robbers to flight after killing at least three of them.

Painting: Dance of the Devadasi

"Be afraid, be very afraid"

– Veronica Quafie

Chapter 10

The Zamindar meets his Nemesis

The Zamindar Shankar Dev Rao a man in his seventies eyed the young and nubile Malli. She was in her late twenties and was much more beautiful than he could have imagined. She was of medium height, hazel nut brown in colour with jet black hair going down to her waist. The zamindar coud make out that her beautifully round breasts were firm and her nipples were erect below the flimsy blouse that she wore. He could imagine how she looked below her pavada which covered a portion of her tummy down to her feet. He had to have her even if that meant the use of brutal force. His wife Yamini Devi in her sixties was a non starter, she was obese with a heart problem and she had rebuffed any attempt by him to have sex with her for the past decade or so. All he could do was to imagine her as a younger person and remember the sex he had with her then and make do with the females his men picked up and forcibly brought to the outhouse. However with his new find Malli all that was about to change, he was on the verge of growing younger after tasting Malli. She was a different proposition altogether, she was not just young but she radiated a kind of youthful vigor and vitality that he felt would serve to rejuvenate his mind and body. For the zamindar neither youth, nor success was enough, for him even at this age, enough was not enough and for him wealth and sex was like sea water, the more he drank it, the thirstier he became. This apart to the zamindar, money was not only the object but also the fountainhead of greed.

Malli and her paramour claimed that they came from a far off land and that they wanted to meet the zamindar to sell something which they felt the zamindar would be interested in buying. They did not mention that both of them were from the fabled kingdom of the Sun God, where because of their amorous relationship, her paramour Muthu, a married man with a wife and two children would have most certainly been fed to the living God and because she was in a sexual relationship with him, she would have been banished from the kingdom into the jungles. Under the circumstances as soon as the two of them realised that their hidden relationship had been discovered, they stole a big bag full of diamonds from the wealthy merchant for whom they worked, collected several blood red ruby like seeds each the size of a small bird's eggs, except for one which was much bigger almost the size of a hen's egg and escaped from the kingdom of the Sun God through the tunnel which over a period of time they had painstakingly discovered so that, in case an eventuality arose they knew how to escape. Their reason for meeting the zamindar was to try and dispose off the diamonds and if possible find a means of livelihood in Mahadevpalli.

Shankar Dev Rao had already eyed Malli as she walked up the numerous flights of stairs that led upto the mansion which was built on a mound, he had also seen Muthu who was accompanying Malli. After seeing the diamonds and after taking a closer look at Malli the zamindar decided that he wanted the diamonds as much as he wanted Malli, the only problem as far as he could see was Muthu. Muthu was the proverbial thorn, before he could lay his hands on Malli. He would have to be taken care of, this the zamindar ensured by waylaying both Malli and Muthu, with his chosen henchmen, when both of them were going back that very night to a house which the zamindar had magnanimously given them to stay for the night, until a better place could be arranged the next day. Muthu was clubbed to death by the zamindar's henchmen and his body was burried under a pile of rocks. Malli was gagged and brought back to the zamindar's estate and locked up in the outhouse, which the zamindar used for meeting women of ill repute or anyone else whom he fancied, away from the gaze of his wife. No one was allowed access to this outhouse and only his closest confidants were allowed to enter it. What went on inside that outhouse was not known to anyone, but, over a period of time, the people who worked in the zamindar's house or on the sprawling orchard around it, came to realize that it was a outhouse which was best avoided, a place which even in broad daylight evoked fear. In this outhouse the zamindar kept Malli in bondage.

On a stiflingly hot day, the zamindar after a whole afternoon of carousal and heavy drinking with his cronies in the outhouse entered the bedroom and eyed Malli who was sitting with her legs folded up in the middle of a massive and ornately designed rosewood bed. The zamindar found her ravishingly beautiful and her hourglass figure irresistible, but she ignored him and this infuriated him to no end. He got up and stripped off his clothes, she knew what was coming and tried to slither away to the further end of the bed when in one lunge he caught her by her legs and drew her back to the centre of the bed. He moved his hands up her legs to her inner thighs and squeezed them causing her excruciating pain, she wept and cried loudly. Then he pulled off her clothes, straddled her legs and kissed her lustily on her stomach while kneading her breasts and tweaking her nipples before parting her legs and entering her repeatedly. There was no love, no tenderness, no time for foreplay and sexual arousal, it was purely an act which was meant to cater to his carnal desire for her as and when he fancied her and to humiliate her since he felt she was not willingly succumbing to him.

This went on for a long time, then one day after forcing himself on her, contrary to the way such encounters ended with Malli weeping and sulking, she suddenly seemed to have a change of heart and said "pedda dora I have a secret to tell you provided you treat me better, I know that Muthu is not coming back, I feel my future is with you, so I have decided not to resist you any longer". Shankar Dev Rao replied "how I treat you will depend on what secret you are holding, which you want to share with me". Malli said "pedda dora I can make you rich beyond your dreams, so rich that kings to whom you are paying obeisance will be in awe of you". Shankar Dev Rao asked "how is that possible? Malli said I know a vidhi ie a method which will make the blood ruby like seeds germinate, when they germinate it will bring untold wealth to you and to your household." By this time Shankar Dev Rao was very interested and he asked "I will treat you with a lot of care from henceforth, but you must reveal the secret". Malli said "on a full moon night you and your family members including all those who work in your house or in any capacity on your sprawling estate must install a stone statue of the Goddess Kali inside your house and after saying your prayers offer the Goddess the blood ruby like seeds, each the size of a small bird's egg soaked in the blood of an animal that has been slaughtered that very night, then you must cook and eat the flesh of the animal you sacrificed. The single big hen's egg sized blood ruby like seed you will keep locked in an iron chest covered in kumkum or vermilion powder. After the pooja you must ask your family members, to plant the blood ruby like small egg shaped seeds, next to all the windows of your house on the ground floor and in a parallel row along the outer wall". Shankar Dev Rao left the outhouse in an extremely upbeat frame of mind, after promising Malli that he would return the following day with many new sets of clothing and jewellery for her to wear. After the zamindar left Malli sat close to the window for a very long time looking at the moon through the open window, she had a peculiar smile on her face.

Back in the house the zamindar wasted no time in finding out the next date on which a full moon could be seen. The zamindar hoped that he would be a king and for that purpose he wanted to build a kingdom. The next morning he sent his men to the neighboring villages to find a sculptor who could make a stone statue of the Goddess Kali. Then the zamindar assembled all the household members and informed them about what he had learnt of recent. Bukka could not contain his excitement and he said "we will be rich, richer than kings". Rudra said "let us not waste time, pedda nana we must plant the seeds immediately after pooja on the next moonlit night". Vikram Dev Rao and his family members were not all that certain of the outcome, they chose to remain silent. Both Yamini Devi and Bukka's wife Parvathi Devi felt that nothing should be done in haste and they wanted to know from Shankar Dev Rao, how he came to know the vidhi ie the method to be used for sprouting the seeds. However, their objection was brushed aside by Bukka, who said "who cares about who gave nana the vidhi, what matters is that it will bring wealth to each one of us". A short while later Yamini Devi called Parvathi Devi to her room and said "I am not at all happy with the way this pooja is being done, I have always been a woman with an independant mind and something tells me that the outcome of this pooja may not be what we have been given to understand. I know that nothing comes free, everything has a price, wealth does not come so easily and if it does, then the cost of acquiring such wealth is usually prohibitive". Parvathi Devi said "amma, I will keep whatever you said in mind but it is my husband I am worried about, I hope he does not insist on my presence".

A few days later, a jatha ie a group of Naga sadhus visited the zamindar who treated them with great respect, the naga sadhus in turn asked the zamindar whether he wanted anything. The zamindar said "can you tell me my future?", one among the sadhus, their head said "do you really want to know the future?, there are times, when it is better that the future remains hidden". Shankar Dev Rao said "I was told that in the near future, I am going to become extremely wealthy along with my family. I want to know whether that is true or false". The naga sadhu told the zamindar zamindar "I will place 9 betel leaves in front of 9 members of your family, then each member, on their own will rub a piece of lime on each betel leaf. After that, each member of your family will drop a speck of water from the river Ganga on the betel leaf". The zamindar was curious and he asked what would happen. The naga sadhu replied "the betel leaves of those who are destined to become rich will turn purple in colour", Shankar Dev Rao asked "what about those whose betel leaf does not turn purple?". The naga sadhu replied "I do not know, it will depend on the colour". The zamindar was not the one to keep quiet, he said "what if it turns red?". The sadhu replied "that person is in great danger". As suggested by the sadhu a betel leaf was placed before each family member and the tantric vidhi or the occult method was used to find out what the zamindar wanted to know. The betel leaves of every one barring that of Shankar Dev Rao, Bukka, Parvathi and Rudra turned purple. The betel leaves in front of them did not change colour, the naga sadhus and their guru looked perplexed, then very slowly each betel leaf which did not change color slowly crumpled, it was as if the life sustaining sap in each leaf had been drawn out. The naga sadhus got up, gave Shankar Dev Rao, Bukka, Parvathi and Rudra a tayathu ie a talisman, to wear at all times and without a backward glance left the house. They sensed the presence of something malevolent, something evil. Parvathi wanted to wear the tayathu but Bukka took it away from her saying "I do not believe in this nonsense", then he picked up all the four tayathus and flung them out of the window.

A few days later on a full moon night Shankar Dev Rao asked his family members to assemble for the puja, in accordance with the tantric vidhi ie method, which he had learnt from Malli (obviously, he did not tell anyone that the source of this information was Malli). Yamini Devi, Vikram Dev Rao and his family did not attend the pooja, because they were not certain of its outcome and they did not want to involve themselves in anything which was incorrect or wrong, Parvathi Devi also wanted to avoid doing the pooja, but never the less she participated in the pooja only because Bukka insisted that she should be present and take part in the pooja, despite Yamini Devi's word of caution. A section of the household staff who felt apprehensive also avoided taking part in the pooja on some pretext or the other.

On completion of the puja, Shankar Dev Rao distributed the seeds to be planted by those who had taken part in the pooja. Bukka said "give two or three seeds nana ", he thought by planting more seeds he would be richer than the rest, not to be outdone, Rudra said "pedda nana give me at least six, I want to plant them", out of the six seeds, he gave Maya two, to plant, so that she also became rich, then he could marry her without any objection from anyone.

While planting the seeds Parvathi Devi noticed that there was a stillness in the air, the birds had stopped chirping and somewhere in the distance she could hear a pack of dogs howling, a scorpion which had been disturbed when someone dug a hole to plant a seed, did not sting that person, instead, it hastily scurried away as if it wanted to get away from something far more sinister which was taking shape. A large flock of birds which used to nest in the mango trees on the estate suddenly created a huge ruckus and flew away, even the fruit eating bats and the normally active owls were conspicuous by their absence. The lamp light Parvathi Devi had brought with her flickered and went out and she suddenly felt very cold despite the fact that it was a very hot and unpleasant night.

That night Rudra came to Vikram Dev Rao's room and said his mother was very ill. Maheshwari Devi rushed to Parvathi's bed side and found that she had high fever and was blabbering someting reapeatedly which sounded like "you...youu..have released me, youuu...will...obey me". Maheshwari Devi said "open your eyes Parvathi". There was no response. Then for a fraction of a second she opened her eyes when Maheshwari Devi was not looking at her, the pupils of her eyes which in human beings is round had condensed into a spindle shape like that of a nocturnal feline, which is able to expand or contract the pupils depending on its necessity to see clearly at night. The next day and in the days thereafter during the day Parvathi Devi behaved in a perfectly normal way, but as soon as it became dark she spent time alone by herself in her bed room. At times, she said she was unwell, at other times she said she was tired. She avoided meeting anyone and she stopped lighting the lamps in her room after it became dark, it was as if she was perfectly at home in the darkness.

Painting: The Pilgrimage

Chapter 11

A Marriage in the Family

The marriage of Lakshmi Devi and Arjun Dev Rao was performed in a holistic manner in the zamindar's mansion in Mahadevpalli, taking into consideration both Marathi and Telugu traditions, given the fact that the zamindar Shankar Dev Rao traced his family roots to the period of Chatrapati Shivaji. The roka or the marriage ceremony which was in keeping with Marathi traditions began with sakhai or sweets. Then the groom's mother Bhramaramba Devi applied haldi kumkum on Lakshmi Devi's forehead as blessings in keeping with tradition and gifted her sarees, jewellery and sakar puda or sweets. The mother of the bride Maheshwari Devi also followed the same ritual with the Arjun Dev Rao. Then both Lakshmi Devi and Arjun exchanged rings. The engagement or nischitartham was celebrated mostly in accordance with Marathi traditions.

Prior to fixing the muhurtam, the bridegroom performed two rituals called snatakam and kasi yatra in keeping with Telugu traditions at his own residence in Rajanpalli. Thereafter the muhurtam was finalised (auspicious day and time of the wedding was fixed), the couple was blessed by elders belonging to both the families. Suhasanies or sumangalis ie married women were invited by Bhramaramba Devi to start making turmeric powder and a powder of pulses and spices called sandega in a mortar and pestle to be used later on in the wedding. Then all the women collectively held a rukhvat exhibiting bridal sarees, jewellery, kitchen utensils, sweets and all sorts of bridal trousseau as part of the rituals. The entire house in Mahadevpalli was decorated with a variety of flowers such as jasmine, rose, chrysanthemum, lotus, marigold, lily, kewda and hibiscus arranged in various patterns along with mango leaves. The pelli or wedding was considered the strongest social bond and involved the merging of two souls, in those days "marriage was a family union and not an individual formality". A few days prior to the wedding, both the families performed a puja for their Kuladevta or family deity followed by having meals for which only family members and close relatives were invited. (Colourful tents were pitched on the lawns outside the zamindar's residence in Mahadevpalli to accommodate guests from near and far who were not directly related to the family of the bride or the groom).

On the wedding day both Lakshmi Devi and Arjun took an auspicious bath to purify both body and soul and prepare themselves for the sacred rites called mangala snanam or abhyangana snanam. The same married women ie suhasanies or sumangalis, who participated in the muhurta karane or fixing the muhurtam, applied turmeric paste using mango leaves on the forehead, shoulders, hands and feet of Arjun Dev Rao. Then the same turmeric paste was taken and applied on Lakshmi

Devi. The abhyanagana snaana (ritual bath) that followed is supposed to have a cleansing and purifying effect. Both the bride and the groom performed Ganapati pooja to invoke blessings of Lord Ganesha for their wellbeing. Then the bride performed a Gauri pooja in her house along with family members and relatives.

Thereafter Lakshmi Devi along with ten suhasanis or sumangalis and her parents went to the mandapam where the marriage was to be performed and awaited Arjun's arrival. On his arrival Lakshmi Devi's mother Maheshwari Devi received Arjun with aarthi and sweets, she washed his feet and applied tilak on his forehead. Arjun then entered the mandapam and a curtain was drawn in between the bride and the groom, restricting their vision. The priest chanted sacred vows accompanied by traditional music played by musicians. At the appropriate, auspicious moment the antarpat ie the curtain was removed and the couple exchanged jaimalas and every one of the guests showered them with akshata or whole rice. This was folowed by kanyadanam, a ceremony which involves the handing over of the bride to the care and protection of the groom followed by panigrahanam which means holding hands, Arjun held the hands of Lakshmi Devi and recited mantras. The ritual pravara, which changes the brides gothra (a term that indicates lineage) was performed, henceforth the bride belonged to the groom's gothra and not her father's gothra. As part of the madhuparkam ritual the bride dressed in a white saree with a red border and the groom wore a white dhoti with a red border, white symbolized purity and red represented strength. The final marriage rituals commenced, a sacred fire was lit and the bride offered grains to Agni ie fire, chanting three mantras repeated by the groom. The fourth and final mantra was uttered silently by the bride. After this ritual the bride's parents worshipped the couple as avatars of Lord Vishnu and Goddess Lakshmi and the couple tied a turmeric thread on each other's hands. Finally the groom tied two strings of the mangalsutra each with a golden disc around the bride's neck and put vermilion or kumkum powder on her forehead. Lakshmi Devi and Arjun exchanged garlands and all those who witnessed this occasion came forward to bless the couple and sprinkled flowers and rice coated with turmeric powder on them. Thereafter saying out loud the same wedding vows the couple together encircled the holy fire seven times, this is called sapthapadi. This was followed by Lakshmi Pooja. After the wedding ceremony was completed the newly wedded couple was seated side by side and a lavish meal was served to all the family members, relatives and guests.. (Kansamas or cooks cooked a variety of vegetarian and non vegetarian food along with at least six varieties of sweets for the guests).

Thereafter the couple left for the groom's place in bullock carts and on arrival Bhramaramba Devi welcomed Lakshmi Devi into her house in Rajanpalli and introduced the newly wedded couple to a host of guests. Lakshmi Devi wore a six yard Paithani saree with gold borders instead of a nine yard Navari saree, along with jewellery, a traditional Marathi necklace and a moon shaped bindi on her forehead given to her by the groom's family and Arjun wore a dress given to him by the bride's family. (In those days, the borders of Paithani sarees had borders and a pallu made from pure gold and copper drawn out into fine zari threads. There were two types of borders, the Narali and the Pankhi. The main body of the saree was woven by a weaver but the inlay border paths were done by a master weaver.)

Later on that night after the neem oil lamps had been lit and there was sufficient light, Bhramaramba Devi showed Lakshmi Devi Dharmavaram silk sarees (while sitting on a massive teak wood bed) which she had bought for her, with its heavy, coloured borders accompanied by shaded pallus which enhanced the intrinsically woven golden borders. A typical wedding saree was heavily embroidered using gold threads and was in a combination of yellow and maroon. Many of the sarees had gold plated borders with artwork along with gold brocaded patterns and motifs. The motifs were mainly elephants, peacocks or an aesthetic temple. Lakshmi Devi was overwhelmed and she hugged Bhramaramba Devi, who told her "I have more for you", Lakshmi Devi asked "how many more do you have?" Bramaramba Devi replied "for you there is no limit". Then Bhramaramba Devi placed the Dharmavaram sarees to one side and opened a sandook ie a camphor wood box in which she had placed Kanchipuram or Kanjeevaram Silks made of absolutely pure mulberry silk and pure gold zari with temple borders and floral patterns.

A famous King of the Chola dynasty who ruled Kanchipuram from 985 to 1014 AD took a keen interest in the silk trade and during the period of King Krishna Deva Raya of the Vijayanagara Empire, Telugu speaking weaving communities such as the Devangas and the Saligars migrated to Kanchipuram. Thus began the historical migration of the silk industry in the 15th century. These two communities were acknowledged for their skills in weaving. The Kanchipuram or Kanjeevaram silks bear the images of the scriptures embossed on the stone walls of gigantic temples in the village of Kanchipuram. The zari used in the Kanchipuram or Kanjeevaram silk sarees was a combination of gold and silver ie silver threads coated with gold.

By this time it was time for dinner which consisted of traditional food items and sweets such as motichoor laddoos, nariyal ke laddoos, puran poli, rava laddoos, fried modak stuffed with bottlegourd and mava shrikhand, thalipeeth, ukadi che modak and a variety of other local sweets.

Later that night after a very hectic day, Lakshmi Devi and Arjun retired to their bedroom, they could finally be together. Lakshmi Devi and Arjun changed into simpler clothes and then they lay on their bed. Arjun kissed Lakshmi on her lips, his mouth touched her intimately, then he slowly undressed her and gently ran his hands over her body. He caressed and kissed her on her body and breasts, sucking her nipples until they were wet, stiff and sensitive and ran his tongue up her neck. She reacted by moaning and came closer to him and kissed him in a way that she'd never thought possible. Then he rocked his hips forward probing for her opening, she bucked her hips against him and gasped as he entered her glistening moistness, ripples of pleasure spread from her pulsating core down her thighs and up her belly and back. His quiet gasps in her ear sent her lust spiralling out of control. It was an out of this world sensation of pure joy, absolutely nothing in this world felt as good as the sensation of him slowly sliding into her and pounding her. He groaned, she kissed him an open mouthed invitation, every movement was pulling her closer to him, she shuddered and clutched his shoulders for strength, loosing herself with each thrust and each pumping caress from his manhood until orgasm after orgasm pulsated through her. They made love passionately late into the night until she went into a deep slumber with his hands around her. (They consummated their marriage at an auspicious hour ie when the muhurtam for sobhanam or sexual intercourse was permitted on the first marital night. Sobhanam at this auspicious hour ensured that the garbhadhana or the foetus laying ceremony took place in accordance with the horoscope and the birth star of both the bride and the groom).

Few days later, late in the afternoon after helping her mother-in-law supervise household chores, Lakshmi Devi found time to indulge in a casual conversation with her husband. After sharing with him snippets of her childhood, her friends, her family she suddenly remembered that she had something very important to disclose and then she spoke at length about the tantric ritual, the puja that was performed and the egg shaped blood red ruby like seeds that her grandfather had planted and that for some reason she felt that the planting of those seeds did not augur well for Mahadevpali and the zamindar. She also told her husband that her aunt Parvathi's behaviour throughout the wedding was rather odd in the sense that she kept away from all the ceremonies and festivities on the pretext that she was ill. Lakshmi Devi told Arjun that when it was time for her to leave for her in-law's house in Rajanpalli, Parvathi Devi stood at her window watching what was going on with a lonely, forelorn look. Then she looked at Lakshmi Devi and their eyes met, there was a look of foreboding in Parvath's eyes, as if she anticipated something terrible was going to happen. As Lakshmi Devi was relating her feelings to her husband she was not aware that in reality sinister things were afoot in the zamindar's estate in Mahadevpalli. She did not know at that time that what she felt was not a figment of her imagination, it was real

Chapter 12

The Second Pilgrimage

A couple of months after Lakshmi Devi's marriage, a horse rider from Pune, bringing a letter from Baji Rao Peshwa-I arrived in Mahadevpalli. In the letter Baji Rao spoke about the imminent threat to Pune from the Nizam and the need to deal with the Mughal garrison in Songadh. The great Peshwa wanted all the allies of Chatrapathi Sahu or Sambaji II, the Maratha King at that time, to collect money for buying cannons and other armaments from the Portuguese in Goa. Vikram Dev Rao immediately replied to the letter and said that both he and his son would undertake a journey to Pune with a very large sum of money, he did not specify that the money would be in the form of diamonds, a portion of the diamonds that his father had taken from Malli.

Initially the Marathas had under Baji Rao helped the Nizam, the governor of the Deccan who had revolted against the Mughal rule to fight against the Mughal emperor Muhammad Shah, at the battle of Sakhar Kheda. The Mughal emperor's forces were defeated and the Nizam honoured Baji Rao with a 7000 man mansabdari, an elephant and a fabulously costly emerald set in gold as a pendant. As a result of this victory the

Mughal emperor recognised the Nizam as the de facto ruler of the Deccan, Nizam-ul-Mulk Asaf Jah-I, had carved out an autonomous Kingdom. However the wily and cunning Nizam knew that to carve out a soverign kingdom of his own he would have to deal with the Marathas. In 1725 The Nizam sent his army to clear out the revenue collectors of the Marathas from the Carnatic region. The Maratha confederacy sent out a force under Fateh Singh Bhosle, but they were forced to retreat. The Nizam's forces invaded Pune and then headed out after leaving behind a section of his army under Fazal Beg. The Nizam's forces then marched on, to plunder Loni, Pargaon, Patas and Baramati, using his artillery to decimate the Marathas. Baji Rao, on the other hand retaliated with guerrilla attacks using his trusted lieutenants Malhar Rao Holkar and Ranoji Shinde. He plundered Jalna, Sindkhed and Berar (where the Nizam's forces were stationed) and feigned an imminent threat to Burhanpur. The Nizam forces stationed in Pune immediately left Pune to meet the Marathas at Palkhed about 48 kms north of Aurangabad because the Nizam felt that his artillery would give him a decisive edge over Baji Rao Peshwa's Marathas. This was a costly miscalculation, the Marathas had acquired fleet footed war horses from the Portuguese in Goa and cannons cast by skilled, renegade Portuguese and other European technicians in addition to acquiring muskets using the Diamonds that Vikram Dev Rao and his son Surya Dev Rao had brought and given to Chatrapathi

Sahu or Sambaji II. As a result the Nizam's forces were beaten and the Nizam signed the treat of Shevgaon conceding the right of the Marathas to collect taxes in the Deccan. The Nizam's dream of forming a kingdom inclusive of vast areas in the Deccan had come to an end.

Vikram Dev Rao and his son stayed on, to celebrate Ganesh Chaturthi with the Chatrapathi Sahu of Satara, grandson of the the Maratha Emperor Chatrapathi Shivaji, in Pune after the Nizam's forces had been evicted, as honoured guests of the emperor, Chatrapathi Sahu and Baji Rao Peshwa-I. The Peshwa asked them to stay with him at his residence in Shaniwarwada and on an auspicious day in the Hindu calendar, Chatrapathi Sahu bestowed the zamindari of Dholapur near the Kingdom of Kolhapur on Vikram Dev Rao as a mark of goodwill and tremendous appreciation for the timely financial help rendered by him.

The Peshwas: At this juncture, it is important to pause the narrative to tell the reader more about the rise of the Peshwas who were the Prime Minisers or the Dewans of the Maratha Kings and who later led the Maratha Confederacy till they lost their power to the British East India Company. Shanirwarwada was built by the Peshwa Baji Rao- I. His father Balaji Vishwanath had served as Peshwa to Chatrapathi Sahu earlier on and on his death Chatrapthi Sahu appointed the son of Balaji Vishwanath ie Baji Rao- I who was just 20 years old at that time to succeed his father. Baji Rao Peshwa- I redrew the map of the Maratha Empire, extending it to Bundhelkhand until it reached almost as far as the gates of Delhi. In 1730 Baji Rao Peshwa moved his residence from the old family wada at Saswad to the village of Pune. He selected 5 acres of land and laid the foundation stone of his new estate on an auspicious Saturday ie on Shaniwar, on 10th January 1730. Over the next few years, a two storey palace with three chowks or courts was built. Three years earlier Baji Rao Peshwa married Mastani the daughter of Chhatrasal Bundela, this second marriage to the orthodox brahmins of Pune was not acceptable and to make matters worse the princess was a half muslim. Baji Rao had separate quarters built for his new bride and when he found that this did not ease the existing situation in any way, he built a separate residence for her in Kothrud. In 1740 Mastani is supposed to have died after Baji Rao's death but there are unconfirmed stories that she was put to death along with her infant son. Under Baji Rao Peshwa's son Balaji Baji Rao or Nanasaheb, the Maratha Empire rose to its zenith, stretching from Attock in present day Pakistan to Thanjavur in present day Tamil Nadu. The Marathas went from being invaders to rulers, requiring to hold territory in the vast expanses of the north, artillery became all the more important. The old notions about soldiers considering life in the artillery as something inferior could not continue.

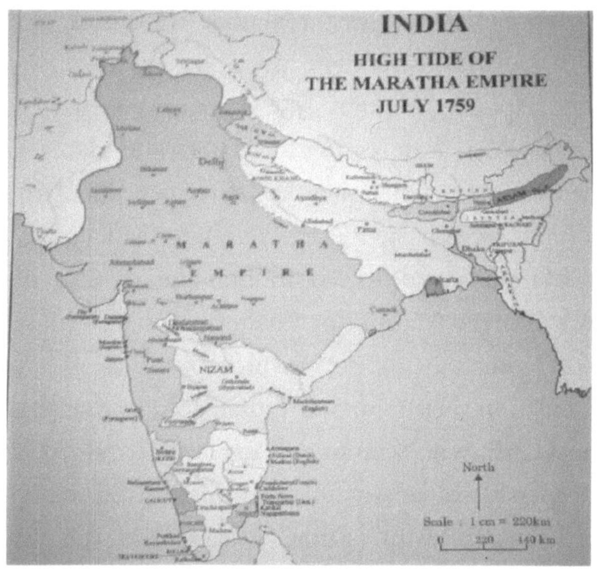

The Maratha Empire

Baji Rao Peshwa had established a factory to produce cannons in the 1730s. Even so, the Marathas lacked the expertise to build and operate the latest guns, primarily because they were a product of the industrial revolution in Europe, which the Marathas had no clue about. Still, considering that they had come into contact with British guns as early as 1660s, it is surprising that they hadn't cracked the code to good artillery even 70 years later, says a lot about both, the Europeans and the Marathas. As a result, the Maratha artillery divisions continued to be manned by Europeans and if not Europeans, then Arabs, Habshis etc.

A Panse or Patwardhan was rare and no match for a Frenchman like a DeBussy or a DeBoigne. Apart from a few sporadic incidents, Marathas continued to be a cavalry centric army right upto the late 1750s. One change happened though. The superiority of the French artillery, which they saw in action at various places, made them induct French trained artillery men like Muzaffar Khan and after him, the famous Ibrahim Khan Gardi. The Marathas endeavored to hire the services of the French General Marquis de Bussy-Castelnau, who served in the Nizam's Army, for training purposes. But when they failed in their efforts, they managed to hire Ibrahim Khan Gardi, who was an artillery expert trained under the leadership of Bussy. The word "gardi" is a corruption of the French word "garde" (guard) and this "gardi" formed the backbone of the Maratha infantry. Udgir in 1760 marked the first time that the Marathas put up a co-ordinated cavalry and artillery attack on the Nizam. The genius of Balwantrao Mehendale ensured a crushing defeat for the Nizam, despite the fact that the Nizam was assisted by the French. Sadly, the Marathas never found the time to perfect this new method and Mehendale died before 14th Jan 1761. The disaster at the battle of Panipat thereafter can be blamed on the lack of co ordination between the artillery and the cavalry.

(The battle of Panipat and its aftermath: The battle of Panipat on the 14thJanuary 1761, is known as the 'the blackest day in Indian history', a day when more than 40,000 Maratha warriors fell on the battle field of Panipat, and more than 20,000 others, mostly women and children, were taken as prisoners. It was a day that changed the course of Indian history and shaped its contours irrevocably.

The battle between the Marathas under Sadashiv Bhau and the Afghans under Ahmad Shah Abdali was a political war between the two powers of the time, the Marathas and the Afghans. The Marathas had arrived at their zenith by 1760, reaching as far in Attock in the west and Calcutta in the east. Its rise was a direct threat to Abdali and created resentment among the local rulers of north India, especially because of their imposition of the levies of 'chauth' and 'sardeshmukhi'. The Rohilla Afghan chiefs of north India, led by Najib–ud-Daulah, invited Abdali, to come to India and wage a 'jehad'. The battle was perhaps India's greatest military disaster and the darkest day in Indian history. Who knows what would have happened had the Marathas won or if they had not ventured out so far from their own homeland without resources or allies. **The British East India Company would not have been able to make inroads so easily if Maratha power remained and India would have been spared 190 years of loot and depredation**. The Rajputs, Jats, Sikhs, Shuja-ud Daulah and other Indian rulers did not join the Marathas in their battle against the outsider. Instead the Indian rulers, including the Rajputs actually invited Ahmad Shah Abdali to their homeland to defeat the Marathas. He merely exploited the divisions within and walked off with the spoils of war.

After the battle of Panipat, Madhavrao–I went about trying to rebuild the Maratha confederacy. He paid special attention to guns and cannons. A factory for making cannon balls was established at Ambegaon near Otur (Junnar) and also a workshop for producing cannons was set up at Pune in 1769. The cannon balls were 7 to 20 sher (1 sher = 1.25 kg). The cannons had colourful names like Jayawanti, Jwalabhavani etc. They played a part in Madhavrao's victory over Haider Ali at Seringapatnam, another ally of the French.

Then in 1818, the British East India Company won a decisive victory against the Marathas in the third Anglo Maratha war and captured Pune and with it Shaniwarwada. The curtains came down on the Marathas when the British exiled the last Peshwa Baji Rao II to Kanpur, the last Peshwa was given just enough time to collecta part of his lavish furnishing and the jewellery he could lay his hands on in Shaniwarwada before going into exile.)

Ganesh Chaturthi was celebrated that year with great fervour in Shaniwarwada in the aftermath of the Nizam's defeat. Vikram Dev Rao and Surya Dev Rao witnessed Ganesh Chaturthi in Pune along with their host Baji Rao Peshwa. Ganesha, Vinayaka known by 108 names is the deva of wisdom (or Ganpati, as known in Marathi) was the family God, or "Kuldaivat' of the Peshwas, the Prime Ministers of the Maratha empire. The festival was celebrated amid much fanfare in the city of Pune, especially at the Shaniwarwada, which was the official residence of Baji Rao Peshwa–I. The festival began on Shukla Chaturthi which is the fourth day of the waxing of the moon and ended on the 14th day of the waxing of the moon known as Anant Chaturdashi.

The ten day period was celebrated with great pomp and show. Men clad in colourful traditional dresses, women wearing gold and pearls from head to toe, a large crowd of devotees assembled to sing 'aarti' for the God of wellbeing, prosperity and happiness. Lord Ganesha's favourite modak (a sweet dish prepared using rice flour stuffed with grated jiggery, coconuts and dry fruits), pooran poli, a variety of laddoos like coconut laddoo, boondi laddoo and karanji or halwa was prepared as naivedhyam or bhog which was distributed as 'prasad' for the family and the visitors to eat.

The Maratha flag was unfurled and in the main durbar hall in Shanirwarwada, towards one corner was a room with a door decorated like the entrance to a temple. The room was lit by lamps and Brahmins conducted the pooja to an idol of Lord Ganesha. Two attendants in a red attire stood outside the doorway. The whole durbar hall was decorated with flowers. Religious and auspicious music was played. Painters were brought to capture the celebration on canvas in the form of paintings which the Peshwa bought. The paintings depicted the grandeur of the event, the colourful clothes and headgear worn by the Peshwa, his family members and all the guests.

In Hindu manuscripts, Lord Ganesha is the younger son of Lord Shiva and Parvati. There are various stories behind his birth, but two of them are the most common ones. According to the first story, Lord Ganesha was created by Parvati out of the paste made of haldi, chandan and flour she applied, before taking mangal snaan i.e purifying bath, on her body. As per the legend Goddess Parvati imagined her child and made a child's figure with the paste and breathed life or praana into this figure. Thus Lord Ganesha came into existence. She gave him the task of guarding her bathroom door while she took a bath. In the meantime, Shiva returned home and Ganesha, who did not know who Shiva was, stopped him. This angered Shiva and he severed Ganesha's head, after a tiff between the two. Parvati was enraged when she came to know about this, Lord Shiva, in turn, promised to bring Ganesha back to life. The Devas were sent to search for a child's head facing north but they could only find an elephant's head. Shiva fixed the elephant's head on the child's body, and that's how Ganesha as seen and revered came into existence. The other popular story is that the Devas requested Shiva and Parvati to create Ganesha so that he can be a Vighnaharta, an avatar for removing obstacles or any kind of hardship and for helping the Devas.

There are four main rituals which are performed during the 10-day long festival, namely Pranapratishtha, Shodashopachara, Uttarpuja and Ganpati Visarjan. The excitement of Ganesh Chaturthi begins in the weeks before the festival actually begins. Artisans start preparing clay idols of Ganesha in different poses and sizes. The Ganesha idols are installed in beautifully decorated 'pandals' at homes, temples or localities. The statue is also decorated with flowers, garlands, chandan, kumkum and jewellery. A ritual called Pranapratishtha is observed where a priest chants mantras to invokeor to infuse life into the idol. Prayers were then offered to Ganesha's idol in 16 different ways. This ritual is called Shodashopachara. People celebrate by singing or playing religious music, dancing to drum beats and by lighting fireworks, all of which added to the festive mood. The Uttarpuja ritual is about bidding farewell to Ganesha with deep respect. This is followed by Ganpati Visarjan, a ceremony wherein the statue is immersed in water while people chanted 'Ganapati Bappa Morya, Purchya Varshi Laukariya' which means 'Goodbye Lord, please come back next year' in Marathi.

In the coming days after Ganesh Chaturthi celebrations in Pune, both Vikram Dev Rao and Surya Dev Rao took leave of the Peshwa and began their journey to the fortress of Songadh via a densely forested area called the Dangs or Dandakaranya so as to avoid the Portuguese forces in southern coastal Gujarat and the British East India Company enscorned in Surat. Enroute they halted to take a hot water bath in the thermal spring in Unai which is considered auspicious by devout Hindus.

In Unai hot water from deep under the ground comes to the top in the form of a spring, the water is very hot and must be mixed with cold water which comes from a nearby water tank so that the temperature comes down to tolerable limits before taking a bath. The water which comes from this underground source is supposed to have a curative property and a bath in this water is meant to rejuvenate the body and remove all tiredness. After bathing in the hot water Vikram Dev Rao, his Son Surya Dev Rao, their body guards from Mahadevpalli and the Peshwa's soldiers who were accompanying them continued on horseback to the Fortress of Songadh to meet Damaji Rao Gaekwad, the conqueror of Baroda.

(**The Gaekwad of Baroda**: The Mughal garrison was defeated and Songadh was conquered by the Maratha general Pillaji Rao Gaekwad, the founder of the Gaekwad dynasty in 1726. The Mughal rule came to an end in the year 1732, when the Maratha general Pillaji Rao Gaekwad once again intensified the Maratha campaigns in south Gujarat and carved out a lineage. His son and successor Damaji Rao Gaekwad defeated the Mughal armies and conquered the state of Baroda in 1734 and during the Golden period of Maharaja Sayajirao Gaekwad III who ruled from 1879 to 1935, the Maharaja greatly contributed to reviving and reforming the state of Baroda by establishing compulsory primary education, libraries and a university. The Gaekwads ruled the princely state of Baroda for over two hundred years till India gained Independance in 1947).

The meeting was sought at the behest of a grateful Damaji Rao Gaekwad for the tremendous financial help rendered by Vikram Dev Rao, who on receiving the letter from Baji Rao Peshwa-I asking for all members of the Maratha Confederacy to collect money to pay the Portuguese to buy horses and to acquire the services of skilled, renegade Portuguese and other European technicians for cannon casting and making cannon balls which were of two types, solid iron balls ie solid shot and exploding iron balls filled with shrapnel, in addition to manufacturing muskets, matchlocks. The money was also needed to make firangi long swords, spears, daggers and to increase the number of Bhimthadi horses which is a cross between the Arabian and a local breed of horses. The Bhimthadi horses were known for their strength, stamina and to be fearless.

A breed of horses called Bhimthadi: A breed of horses, which once served in the Maratha army, but are now on the verge of extinction. The "Deccan Horse", one of the finest cavalry regiments during the British Raj in India relied on these cross bred variety of horses. The Bhimthadi, Gangthadi, Nirthadi was the preferred mount of the Maratha Bargir (cavalryman). Sardar and Warrior of the Maratha Confederacy, Yashwantrao Holkar (1776-1811) always rode into battle on his favourite mare "Mahua", which was of the Bhimthadi breed. Up until the 19th century, the breed was numerous, due to its patronage by Maratha cavalry forces. Chatrapati Shivaji Maharaj was a keen breeder of horses and supplied the Bargirs from the Royal stables. The Maratha Light Cavalry horse was developed from mating the Bhimthadi with Arabian, Persian and Turki Sires with the best of breed coming from the villages near the Bhima and Nira rivers of Pune district. Maratha horsemen dominated large parts of Gujarat and Rajputana in the 18th Century and it is more than likely that they incorporated the Kathiawari and Marwari breeds.

Portuguese Goa Coat of Arms

The Portuguese conquest of Goa in 1510 AD was the first European annexation of Indian Territory since the invasion of Alexander the Great. From Goa the Portuguese war ships with their superior firepower dominated the trade routes. The Portuguese cornered the trade in spices and in horses. Warfare on the Indian mainland was dominated by cavalry. Horses were essential for the armies of the Indian rulers. Very few good horses were bred in India and a large number of horses were imported from Arabia, it was this horse trade that the Portuguese controlled. The Portuguese general Afonso de Albuquerque gave instructions that all war horses coming from Arabia and Persia must be off loaded in Goa. His ships intercepted those ships which carried horses and escorted them to Goa. Those who voluntarily brought horses to be sold in Goa and those who purchased the horses, were given customs concessions on their other cargo. There was no import duty on horses, but a heavy tax was levied on their export out of Goa, this tax eventually brought in over half the revenue of Goa. The King of Vijayanagar and Albuquerque's former enemy, the Adil Shah of Bijapur sent their ambassadors to Goa. The southern Hindus and the nothern Muslims were often at war and both offered their friendship to the Portuguese to secure a monoply over the purchase of horses in Goa. Albuquerque played one against the other and sold horses to both. Albuquerque also secured a pool of resources like rice and revenue to pay the soldiers and sailors. He also acquired skilled native shipwrights and craftsmen capable of building and repairing fleets, apart from gunsmiths, to maintain arsenals with which to arm them, crucial to lessen Portuguese dependence on men and material from faraway Europe and to ensure the Portuguese presence in India for a very long time. Establishing a strong naval base in Goa was vital to undermining Muslim trade in the Indian Ocean, as the Potuguese naval forces could sever the link between the hostile Sultanate of Gujarat and the rich spice producing areas of southern India, where a powerful lobby of Gujarati merchants were inciting the locals to attack the Portuguese.

For the majority of the Potuguese, life in India was not easy. There was a perpetual shortage of men, to man the ships and the army. Few respectable peasants in Potugual or working men volunteered for a life in India, where death was common and rewards uncertain. To find enough men for the overseas empire, convicts and murderers were allowed to avoid execution, if they volunteered for banishment to the East. Wages to be paid to these convicts was deferred until after they arrived in India and for many months thereafter. The penniless unfortunate thieves and pirates entered the private services of the administrators and became thugs, the very same thugs who landed on the Bengal coast and became slave catchers. Very few respectable Portuguese women came to India and to make up the short fall, the Portuguese government officials in Goa, the thugs and the thieves took concubines and women slaves. Thus Goa and the Portuguese renegades in the East ie Bengal, relied on a huge population of slaves whom they married at times. A relatively low ranking Portuguese officer had almost 20 slaves, while a man of substance may have had hundreds. Women slaves were sold naked in open auctions and fetched a higher price if they were virgins. However it goes to the credit of Afonso de Albuquerque that he encouraged his men to marry native Goans. After the battle of Talikota in 1565 AD in which the Vijayanagar Empire was wiped out, the Deccan Sultanates once again united to attack the Portuguese forts. This resulted in a ten month long siege of Goa in 1570 AD. The Portuguese survived the onslaught and continued to control the horse and spice trade. Finally it was in 1961 that the Portuguese state of Goa came to an end and was incorporated into the Union of India.

******

A part of the diamonds brought by Vikram Dev Rao was used by the Marathas under Chatrapathi Sahu and his most trusted advisor and commander Baji Rao Peshwa-I to pay the Portuguese in Goa for war horses and to pay for the services of skilled, renegade Portuguese and other European technicians for casting cannons and manufacturing muskets as mentioned above, which was used to defeat the Nizam's forces, to rout the Mughal garrison in Songadh and finally to drive the Mughals out of Baroda state. The remaining diamonds were sold for a staggering sum of money to the Governor-General of the Dutch East India company (the company was based in Pulicat, Masulipatnam, Bimlipatnam, Jaggarnathpuram and Tranquibar) who paid the Marathas in gold guilders which he received by way of payment from the Dutch Royal Family, minted originally from gold captured by the Dutch Admiral Piet Heyn who captured an entire fleet of Spanish galleons when the fleet was making its way back to Spain carrying tons of gold and silver which the Spaniards had looted from South America, starting with the Spanish conquistadores and the loot of Inka gold.

(Historical perspective: From the 16th to the 18th century, Spanish convoys of ships transported European goods to the Spanish colonies in the Americas and transported colonial products, especially gold and silver back to Spain. Beginning in the 1560's, shipping between Spain and the Americas was organised on a regular basis. In general, two fleets of 30-90 vessels sailed from Sevilla ie "Seville" to the American colonies each year, the flotilla left in spring for the West Indies and Honduras. Another fleet left in August for Catagena, modern day Colombia and Porto Bello (now Portobelo), on the Atlantic coast of Panama. After the winter in America, both fleets returned to Havana, Cuba the following spring and returned to Spain protected by war ships of the formidable Spanish Armada. The immense wealth in gold and silver carried by these ships offered a tempting prize for the English and the Dutch. One such fleet was captured, looted and destroyed by the Dutch Admiral Piet Heyn off the coast of Cuba in 1628, another fleet was looted by the English under the command of Robert Blake in the Azores in 1657).

The Portuguese Governor of Goa Francisco de Almeida on his part presented the diamonds in his possession, the equivalent of a King's ransom to the Portuguese Royal Family. **Two of Europe's biggest Royal Families were wearing diamonds from the Surya Samrajyam or the Kingdom of the Sun God.**

******

After the rout of the Mughals, Damaji Rao Gaekwad decided to build a fortress in Songadh, the fortress was built on top of a hill as a vantage point to keep an eye on enemies. The fort of Songadh literally meant 'fort of gold', "Son" which means gold and "Gadh" which means fortress. In this fortress Damaji Gaekwad met his guests and showed them around the fortress and offered prayers along with his guests at a temple he had constructed, apart from visiting a kund atop the hill within the fortress, the water of this kund or pond tasted like it had natural camphor mixed in it. This was possible because at least three camphor trees were growing near the kund and the roots of the camphor trees were deeply entrenched in the kund. Both Vikram Dev Rao, his son Surya Dev Rao and their host Damaji Gaekwad spent sometime in hunting deer, they had bagged three Chital deer and a Sambhar stag when they suddenly came across a fearsome tiger.

Painting: The King is Dead, Long Live the King

Damaji Gaekwad fired on the brute with his musket but the shot did not kill it, instead it angered the animal and it turned on the Gaekwad, the hunt would have turned into a tragedy but for Vikram Dev Rao's shot, fired at the nick of time from his musket which killed the tiger. After a few days Vikram Dev Rao and his son, took leave of a much indebted Gaekwad, sometime towards the end of the year 1736 and returned to Pune where a letter from his wife Maheshwari Devi awaited him.

******

(**Historical perspective**: It is intresting to note that in 1888 Sayajirao Gaekwad-III a later day descendant, the then ruler of Baroda shot one of the biggest tigers in Songadh which was stuffed and can be seen even today at the Sayajirao Gaekwad-III Museum in Baroda. In another instance when Maharaja Sayajirao Gaekwad–III was on a hunt in Amreli, he fired on a tiger and missed. Two village boys shouted loudly and distracted the tiger, giving Sayajirao the time to reload his gun and shoot down the tiger. Sayajirao Gaekwad–III installed the statues of the two boys from Dhari to express his gratitude to the boys for saving his life).

******

On reading the letter from his wife, Vikram Dev Rao came to know that strange incidents had taken place in Mahadevpalli, a husband and wife pair who stayed in the servant's quarters on the estate said that they had seen something unbelievable. According to them one of the cows which had somehow strayed from the cowshed and was eating some grass was suddenly hamstrung by a number of tentacles or creepers. The couple could not tell definitely what it was that had wrapped itself around the cow, since they were at a great distance. Subsequently the couple looked for the cow, after arming themselves with two stout sticks but there was no sign of the cow. Maheshwari Devi spoke about similar incidents where smaller animals such as a goat or a pig had disappeared. She wanted Vikram Dev Rao and Surya to return as soon as possible. On reading this letter Vikram Dev Rao paid homage to the King Chatrapthi Sahu and Baji Rao Peshwa-I, prior to taking leave of them in Pune, after making the necessary arrangements for his son Surya Dev Rao to stay back and to look after the zamindari in Dholapur which was bestowed on them by King Chatrapathi Sahu.Vikram Dev Rao wrote back to his wife about his plans, about the zamindari of Dholapur which was bestowed on him and about Surya staying back to take care of day to day affairs in Dholapur. In the very same letter Vikram informed Maheshwari that it would take about two weeks to settle matters in Dholapur to his satisfaction then about another three weeks to return.

In the meanwhile back in Mahadevpalli, when Vikram Dev Rao and his son Surya Dev Rao were actively engaged in celebrating Ganesh Chaturti in Pune with King Chatrapathi Sahu and Baji Rao Peshwa-I. On the instructions of Yamini Devi the whole household in Mahadevpalli except Shankar Dev Rao, Bukka and Rudra who dropped out due to some prior commitments and Parvathi Devi who said that she was not well, went on a pilgrimage to Kanipakam and Sri Ardhagiri Anjaneya Swamy Temple located in Aragonda (which from ancient times was very famous for curing skin diseases with the holy water of Sanjeevaraya Pushkarini).

Kanipakam: In Tamil "Kani" means wetland and "Pakam" means flow of water into wetland. According to the legend of the temple there were three brothers and each one had a handicap. One was dumb, the second brother was deaf and the third brother was blind. They were eking out their livelihood by cultivating a small piece of land. One day the water in the well got dried up and they could no longer continue to irrigate their fields. One of the brothers got into the well and started digging the well in the fond hope that there would be water at a greater depth. While digging, his iron implement hit a stone like formation. Later, he was shocked to see blood oozing out from it. Within a few seconds the entire water in the well turned blood red in colour. Simultaneously all the three brothers became normal ie they were no longer handicapped. As soon as the villagers came to know about this miracle, they thronged to the well and tried to deepen the well further. But their attempt proved futile because the 'swayambhu' idol (the self-manifested) of Lord Vinayaka emerged from the swirling waters. The holy water from the well is offered to the devotees as theertham. The swayambhu idol of Kanipakam is the up-holder of truth. Day to day disputes between people is resolved by taking a 'special oath'.

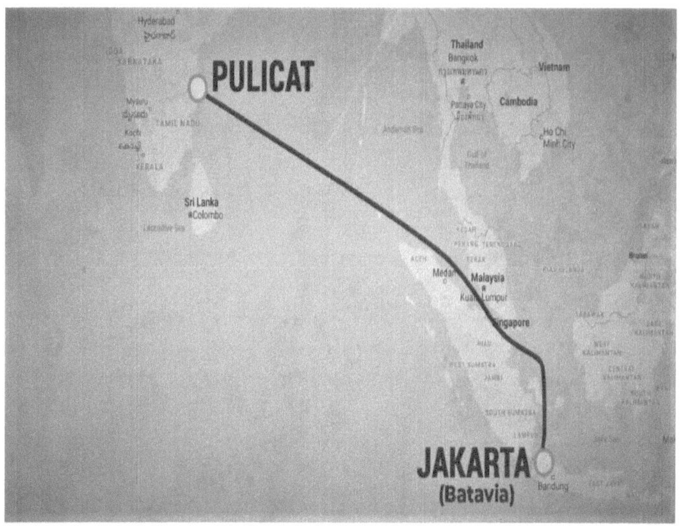

The Slave Trade from Pulicat to Batavia

"I fear not the dark itself, but what may lurk within it ".

– Unknown

Chapter 13

Slave Trade in India and the Zamindar

After forcibly acquiring Malli, Shankar Dev Rao was a man who was looking forward to life, he was a man in a hurry to experience youth once again and was waiting for the seeds, he and a section of his family members had planted to show results. After all Malli had promised him that it would bring him untold wealth and he had no reason to disbelieve her, because she was in his custody and she knew that in case what she said did not turn out just as she predicted, it would cost her dearly. This apart, the diamonds which he had forcibly acquired from her had already made him a fabulously rich man. In the meantime apart from extorting money from the villagers who were a part of his zamindari he had found a new and lucrative source of income, the business of acquiring slaves for the Dutch East India Company surrepticiously, despite a ban on slavery imposed by the British East India Company. The Dutch East India Company was headquatered in very many places in India at that time such as Bimunipatnam, Jaggernathpuram, Tranquibar and Pulicat. Shankar Dev Rao's business was to scout around for young boys and girls, in the age group between 10 to 20, which included, both males and females in good health and to keep a tab on them, through an intricate web of agents and spies. At the opportune moment these males and females were lured with a promise of a job or lured into a bogus marriage or simply abducted and brought to a central staging point by bullock carts by night with their hands tied and their mouths gagged, those who resisted were sedated. After bringing them to a heavily guarded lonely safe house Bukka and his son Rudra picked those who could be sold. The others especially the good looking females were kept as slaves to do their bidding, to be used as dancing girls and to be supplied at times to the officers of the British East India Company to buy their silence and cooperation. Many of these slaves were sold discreetly to the officers and sepoys of the British East India Company, as "bibis or mistresses". These bibis provided the officers with companionship, washed their linen and took care of them when they fell ill. The bibis also proved to be useful keys to the local language and as a go-between for the English Sahab and the local Indians. Many officers learnt Hindustani languages and grammar from their mistresses. The bibis provided the officers and the sepoys a home away from their home in England. The British East India Company tacitly encouraged this kind of a liaison between their officers and local women, on the understanding that the concerned officer or sepoy did not insist on bringing his native "bibi or mistress" back to England. This method was also considered a safer option than to allow the troops to go to local sex workers and run the risk of becoming infected with highly contagious venereal diseases. At the time when the officer or the sepoy finally went back to England they normally left a will. A reading of several wills makes it clear that the relationship between the British colonialists and their native bibis or mistresses was multi faceted, based on every day, intimate interactions, which were not merely sexual. The wills detailed how the bibis became an integral part of the household, providing the British colonialists a manual, sexual and an emotional dimension apart from the reproductive dimension, given the frequency with which the the officer referred to his bibi in the documents as the "beloved, faithful mother of his children". In some of the wills the concerned officer specifically instructed the executors to find a good master for his bibi or mistress after his departure for England because of her "youth, good disposition and because she was the mother of his children". The children, almost always natural or illegitimate born out of this association did not belong to the mother by virtue of being half European, on the paternal side. In the 19th century the colonial state created orphanages and schools for the mixed-race children, who later on swelled the ranks of the Anglo-Indian community in India. It was a well oiled system that thrived on sexual depravity and misery, the zamindar ie Shankar Dev Rao was at the middle of this thriving business.

Dutch East India Company

VOC: At this juncture it is important for me to pause the narrative to give the reader an insight into the activities of the Dutch East India Company or the VOC (Vereenigde Oost Indishe Compagnie or simply the VOC) headquartered in a fortress called the Castle Geldria built after obtaining permission from the Vijayanagara rulers some time in 1610. This fort represented the seat of power of one of the most voracious predators of its kind. The Dutch East India Company which arrived like all seafaring traders on the coast of the Indian sub continent in the 16 the century, first gained control of Masulipatnam or modern day Machilipatnam on the coast of Andhra Pradesh in 1605, then Tegenepatnam (Fort St. David) in 1608, finally making their way to Pulicat or Pazhaverkadu in 1610. Using their superior and better armed ships, the Dutch ousted the Portuguese from Pulicat, which the Portuguese had painstakingly built up from a mere trading post in 1502. Thereafter for two centuries Pulicat was the administrative headquarters of the Dutch in India and the thriving centre for exporting diamonds, extracted and sold by the Guntur and the Golkonda diamond mining company (the diamonds mined were blue, pink and the rare Type IIa, only 1% of the diamonds mined were of this calibre, there were 38 diamond mines in total of which 23 mines were in Golkonda and the remaining in Bijapur) which was owned by the fabulously rich Nizam of Hyderabad. Smaller quantities of diamonds were sourced by individuals from the banks of the Krishna River along with Type IIa diamonds from the Kingdom of the Sun God which had an exceptional limpid quality and contained no measurable trace of nitrogen (which is responsible for the yellow tinge in diamonds). These diamonds epitomized the perfect amalgamation of beauty with rarity (however the inflow of diamonds from the Kingdom of the Sun God was a mere trickle, most people in the 18th century even doubted that the diamonds came from the Kingdom of the Sun God). Jean Baptiste Tavenier in an account of his voyages has stated that India had extensive deposits of diamonds in Rayalseema and a few other places. The most iconic natural diamonds mined from the Guntur and the Golkonda mines was the Kohinoor diamond, the Dresden Green diamond, the Regent diamond, the Noor-ul-Ain diamond, the Nassak diamond, the Orlov diamond and the infamous Hope diamond, a diamond which contrary to its name left all those who bought and possessed it,"hopeless and destitute".

The Dutch East India Company also exported thousands of barrels of spices such as nutmeg, cloves and pepper to various overseas destinations. In addition to all these activities The Dutch East India Company had also set up a gun powder manufacturing unit in Pulicat which established their hegemony in the 17th century over vast parts of eastern and southern India which came to be known as the "Dutch Coromandel".

Slavery: Apart from all this business there was a more lucrative and sinister business in which they were involved, the business of capturing free individuals, both men and women who were forcibly transported to far off lands especially Jakarta, 'modern day Indonesia', known as Batavia in those days, where they worked as slaves ie bonded labourers, on vast plantations. Wil O Dijk, an independant researcher was the first person to throw light on this notorious, murky business which the Dutch East India Company or the VOC indulged in, based on her painstaking research of VOC files available with the National Archives of the Netherlands, in her research paper titled "The Dutch Trade in Asian Slaves, Arakan and the Bay of Bengal, 1621-1665". The Dutch obtained slaves from Bengal on the eastern coast, (the Northern Burmese Kigdom of Arakan raided the Bengal coast and captured a large number of Bengalis, these Bengalis were sold in Pulicat) from locations like Masulipatnam, Bimunipatnam in modern day Andhra Pradesh and from Caracal or Karaikal, Tondi and Adirampattinam in Tamilnadu and transported them to their headquarters in Pulicat at the edge of a vast lagoon, where they were sold to prospective buyers and sent to Batavia, Mauritius and Reunion to work as plantation labourers. Even today standing at the water's edge with your eyes scanning the horizon, one can imagine galleons sailing into the lagoon from the open sea, imagine the flotilla slowly inching towards the shore to pick up a grim cargo of human slaves, shackled, partially dressed or wholly naked columns of young men and women. It is estimated that close to 50,000 Indian slaves were shipped to Jakarta ie Batavia).

Many hundreds, if not thousands, of Indians, mainly from Bengal, the Coromandel Coast and Kerala were taken to the Cape ie South Africa and sold into slavery. Officers of ships and officials of the Dutch East India Company returning to Holland usually took slaves or servants with them and sold them at high profit in the Cape. Slaves could not be taken to Holland where slavery was prohibited. Many others were carried by Danish and British ships. While most of the Indians were taken from Dutch trading posts in India, a considerable number were also taken from Batavia, as thousands of Indians had been taken by the Dutch as slaves to Batavia. Some of these early slaves from India especially women from Bengal who were acquired by senior officials of the Dutch East India Company for domestic work were relatively fortunate. The great majority of those enslaved in the Cape lived under miserable conditions. Many of those sold in the Cape, however, had not been slaves in

India, but domestic servants, bonded or otherwise and in a lot of cases Indian natives from Bengal and other parts of India who came to the Cape as free servants, were bartered or sold to the colonists "(Slavery at the Cape of Good Hope 1831)".

There is reason to believe that many of the slaves were children, even less than ten years old, who had been kidnapped in India. Warren Hastings, the then British Governor General of British India, wrote "the practice of stealing children from their parents and selling them as slaves has long prevailed in this country and these children are conveyed out of the country on the Dutch and French vessels".

Pulicat became a centre for slave trade because it was located at the mouth of a lagoon, it was considered as one of the few good natural harbours on the eastern coast of India. One of the earliest references to Pulicat is in the 1st century AD in the Roman manual "The Periplus of the Erythrean Sea", which mentions that Pulicat was one of the finest sea ports. In the 15th and the 16 th centuries under the Vijayanagara Empire, Pulicat reached its zenith in wealth and fame. It was a hub for exporting textiles such as calico to Burma and South East Asia, as well as a cutting and polishing centre for Golconda and other diamonds and Burmese blood rubies. In 1619 the Dutch East India Company sacked and destroyed the Javanese capital of Jakarta and in its place they built a new settlement called Batavia.The Dutch expelled the native Javanese and forbade them from entering Batavia and then they began to import slaves from India to work in their factories, warehouses, plantations and homes. They also imported African slaves from Portuguese controlled Mozambique but this proved to be unviable as most of the African slaves died because of terrible conditions out at sea and during the long sea voyage, under the circumstances the import of slaves from India was the only viable option. The cost of a slave from India ranged from 27 to 40 guilders when the demand was very high and as little as 4 guilders when the demand was sluggish. In this entire skullduggery, the zamindar of Mahadevpalli was an able partner and an ally of the Dutch and they rewarded him handsomely for the services he rendered and for keeping the trade alive, inspite of the official ban imposed on slavery by the British East India Company as already mentioned.

There was also a large demand for African slaves known as "Coffree or Kafri" in some port towns, they were brought all the way from West Africa around the Cape of Good Hope to India and other South East Asian countries. Apart from the Dutch, throughout the 18th century the British East India Company in Bombay procured slaves from Africa, mainly from the slave markets in Zanzibar either for their own use or for onward transmission to the East Indies where the company had factories. Bombay was the clearing house for slaves imported from Africa. It was only in 1813 that the import and export of slaves was forbidden, but the penalty for any violation was low, as a result it was frequently violated. The citizens of Bombay, both Indian and European, owned slaves were a part of their household. When Dady Nusserwanjee (1734-1799) made his will he settled minor bequests on his six African slaves (or Siddi, as they were called in Bombay) and instructed his son Ardaseer Dady to arrange for the male slaves to be married. Finally in 1837 slavery was officially outlawed by the British Parliament, except for the territories governed by the British East India Company, including Ceylon and the South Atlantic Island of St.Helena. The British East India Company lobbied the British Parliament and convinced the law makers that what existed in territories under the company in South Asia was "free labour" and not slavery. Outlawing slavery in India however did not have an immediate effect or impact and slavery in various forms persisted in Bombay and elsewhere in India right upto the end of the 19th century and continued thereafter as perpetual debt–bondage, where bonded labour continued in perpetuity against the non-payment of a debt.

The third centre in India in the 18th century in which an active slave market existed was in Calcutta. These slaves brought by the Portuguese and Burmese traders and pirates, were actively sold throughout Calcutta, mostly on the riverfronts. Budge Budge for example was a place south of Calcutta where Portugese slave ships moored after their shipments were brought to Calcutta by road or by small boats. The Bay of Bengal was a hot bed of pirates from various nations, the most notorious were the Burmese, followed by the Portuguese and the Dutch, who plundered merchant vessels in the Bay of Bengal and sold the survivors into slavery. The "harmads" carried out frequent raids and plundered the coastal communities of eastern Bengal. The word harmad is a colloquial distortion of the Potuguese and the Spanish word "armada", fleet of warships. In Bengal the word came to be synonymous with slave raiding Portuguese. The attacks were carried out essentially by Potuguese privateers and adventurers from their flotillas, often in collaboration with the Mogs ie Burmese or the Arakenese. The slave trade in Bengal was characterised by the presence of Portuguese privateers consisting of freebooters, convicts and adventurers who came to make their own fortune, away from the stifling official structures located on the west coast of India ie the Portuguese rulers of Goa, the Estado. The eastern part of India for the Harmads was their "shadow empire". The privateers began settling in Bengal for numerous reasons, such as to escape judicial action for crimes committed, to evade religious persecution spearheaded by the growing power of the inquisition in Goa or simply to make more money in criminal and uscrupulous ways. The slave markets became so famous that Mughal Emperor Shah Jahan wiped out one of the most notorious Portuguese pirate nests on the Bengal coast, so as to prevent the depopulation of coastal Bengal. Sometimes even commercial vessels of the French, the English and the Dutch went "rogue" and plundered the Bengal and the Andhra coastal countryside, imprisoning men and women. These captives were sold off in various ports and ended up as cooks, barbers, coach drivers, entertainers, ayahs etc. or they ended up as domestic servants in the houses of Englishman and their English wives who had enriched themselves in India and were called "Nabobs and Nabobinas" (in India the word Nawab is used as a title, the Englishman and their wives who became very wealthy in India were called "Nabobs" and their wives were called "Nabobinas", both the words originated from the word "Nawab").

Lastly there was a small but thriving market for impoverished Anglo-Indian slaves and penniless English slaves, who, because of their precarious economic and social conditions, voluntarily entered the slave market ie sold themselves into slavery and made their services available for some sort of security, that ensured that they would be fed and housed by their masters.

(Historical perspective: On Goree Island**,** 3 kms off the coast of the city of Dakar, in Senegal, Africa, there is a museum and a memorial to the Atlantic slave trade. The museum attracts thousands of visitors from around the world, who came here to pay their respects in a place that served as the final departure point for slaves in Africa. Sadly, no such monument commemorates Indian slaves, who were captured and transported to the corners of the world, going even as far as the Caribbean islands).

Zamindars like Shankar Dev Rao profiteered immensely by funding the import and export of African slaves in the 18th century. They worked as financiers for the import and export of African slaves for the British, the Dutch, the French Company of the East Indies (Compagnie Francaise des Indes Orientales) and the Portuguese East India Company, from time to time and not merely as procurers of Indian slaves for the Dutch East India Company. In this business Shankar Dev Rao was ably assisted by his son Bukka and his grandson Rudra. Vikram Dev Rao was not a part of this racket because his mother Yamini Devi who he was very fond of, forbade him from having anything to do with the slave business.

Dancing "Natch" Girls

Chapter 14

An Untimely End

On this full moon night, like on previous full moon nights Shankar Dev Rao walked around his vast mango estate, then he decided to have a bath in a pond which was at some distance from his vast mansion. Nobody would come to this pond and most people knew that the zamindar was in the habit of swimming in this pond, it was one among his favourite pastimes, the other being the time he spent with Malli. With his mind on Malli the zamindar took off his clothes, he was not aware that his movement was being closely monitored. After a while the zamindar settled into a shallow end of the pond with half of his body under water and dozed off. Then suddenly he felt like very strong creeper/vine like appendages were entwining themselves around him. He was a very strong man and he was used to being surprised by his enemies. The zamindar in a flash, reached out for his sword which he always carried with him and slashed at the creepers or vines that were wrapping themselves around him. With great difficulty he cut them down and extricated himself from whatever was trying to wind itself around him but not before being hurt greviuously from multiple cuts and puncture marks made by suckers which tore away small chunks of his skin and the underlying flesh and tissues. He was also losing a lot of blood. Inspite of all these injuries, the zamindar somehow dragged himself out of the pond and staggered back to his mansion where his guards rushed to his aid. Then the village doctor was called for and he applied some kind of a medicinal paste to the wounds and bandaged them. A short while later the zamindar developed a very high fever. Bukka, Rudra and the female members of the family rushed to be with the wounded zamindar. Later that night the zamindar of Mahadevpalli died. His body was wrapped and kept in the middle of a room. Since it was stiflingly hot, the window was kept open, ironically it was the same window beneath which the zamindar had planted one of the blood ruby like small egg shaped seeds which in the past few months had grown prodigiously. A guard was kept on duty to keep a watch on the dead body and to ensure that the lamp placed at the head of the body did not die down. Sometime during that night the guard went to attend the call of nature, when he returned, the zamindar's body had disappeared, only the white shroud ie the white cloth which was wrapped around the dead body was lying on the floor. The matter was brought to the notice of Bukka and Rudra immediately, both of them did not waste time in launching a massive manhunt, in the hope of catching the person who had the body of the late zamindar, but they found nothing despite hours of searching. It was as if the late zamindar did not exist at all. Bukka was livid and in the morning he undertook another search. Each and every corner of the vast estate was searched but this search like its predecessor did not produce any result. In the days to come Bukka and Rudra let loose a reign of terror, they even announced that a large bounty would be paid to anyone for any information that could lead to the recovery of the late zamindar's body and for any information regarding the individual or group of individuals responsible for the dastardly act. Unfortuately this did not bring forth the desired result but Bukka continued with his uncouth methods to worm out information, with no success.

Bukka's cruelty was like every other vice, it required no motive except the opportunity to inflict pain on others. With Bukka a vast majority of people lived in both physical and mental misery. Bukka was a man who lived with a stigma that he was the child of a woman who was initially the zamindar's keep, whom the zamindar married at a much later point of time ie after his birth, this left him with a deep sense of inferiority and shame, which manifested itself, in the form of ruthlessness to others. Bukka was evil because he treated his fellow human beings as things and believed that human beings could be controlled by bestial acts imposed on them.

In the days following his father's death Bukka went beserk, first and foremost he could not understand how his father a very strong man died, secondly he was in a quandary about the disappearance of his father's body from his father's own bed room, where it was under watch throughout the night except for a very short period when whoever was watching over the dead body had gone for a short while to attend to nature's call. Bukka was at his wits end and had come to the conclusion that there was an element of foul play in his father's death. To try and ferret out the perpetrators, Bukka rounded up his enemies and their families and made them stand under the sun for hours on end without food and water. He would tap a woman standing in the line who may have been a wife, a sister or the mother of someone who Bukka did not like, the person who Bukka tapped would step out of the line and strip naked, this was done to humiliate them in public. In case Bukka took a fancy to any particular female he took her to a heavily guarded, isolated house atop a small hillock overlooking the vast plains of Rayalaseema called the Shakuntala Villa, a place of sexual legend which made even the most debauched zamindars in Rayalaseema and its surrounding areas blush. After a couple of days it became evident that nothing regarding his father's death and the subsequent disappearance of his body could be determined from these people. Then Bukka applied even harsher measures to make anyone who had any knowledge with regard to his father's death reveal the truth by picking five people at random and flogging them. This went on for a full month, in some cases the poor victims succumbed to their injuries. Finally when all the methods drew a blank he had a few unfortunate victims thrown into a pit with ravenously hungry dogs to be torn to shreds while others were forced to watch the ordeal. At the end of this marathon exercise nothing emerged which could cast any light on his father's strange and untimely death and the even stranger disappearance of his father's body on the very night he died. It was beginning to look as if his father's death was caused by dark and sinister forces much beyond Bukka's or for that matter any human control.

Chapter 15

The ill-begotten Son

Bukka had another weakness, his relationship with women of ill repute and his frequent visits to the houses of such women. Many of those whom he visited were trained singers and dancers and a visit to such a person's house included more than sexual gratification. Bukka's inability to abstain from visiting houses of ill reputation and his dependance on prostitute-mistresses as an indispensible form of entertainment made it difficult for him to reform. In the brothels he was plied with food, drinks, drugs, all manners of addictive substances and could engage in all kinds of debauchery that had the effect of overwhelming his senses, the mistresses in turn exploited their unrestrained customers/paramours.

In those days prostitutes as a category had number of subcategories. A Swairini was a married woman who prostituted herself in her own or some other house and whose husband was powerless against her, she could snub him on his face. A Kulta was a married woman who secretly and occasionally slipped out of her house to enjoy the embraces of one or more lovers. She was afraid of her husband and his relatives and went astray not so much for the sake of money but for love, romance and to satisfy her lust. The Nati was a prostitute who professedly lived by dancing, music and acting on the stage and had a fixed 'man', with or without whose approval, she entertained people of her choice and earned money. The Ganikas were professional prostitutes. They were the highest in the rank of prostitutes and were well known for their good manners and deportment. A Muhuttika was a girl of pleasure engaged for a short duration who attracted men by her tempting figure and voice. Until recently, in India prostitution was considered and dealt with as a criminal offence, whereas, as early as in the 18th century prostitutes were accepted as a necessary part of Indian society and the high and mighty flirted or had relationships with them. These extramarital relationships were openly flaunted and those who indulged in it considered it as a symbol of their manliness and financial capacity.

The patronage of stalwarts like Bukka gave the mistresses a position and power in society which became a viable occupation for destitute women from diverse backgrounds. These women were able to cater to a new type of clientele, who were products of the colonial order. Although Bukka indulged in extramarital affairs which hurt and humiliated his wife Parvathi, he feared the sullying of her honour and made every effort to ensure that she remained insulated and protected from other marauders like himself by keeping her in zanana, behind a veiled purdah.

For Bukka cuckolding offered a greater pleasure than maintaining a relationship with unmarried women and prostitutes because he derived a sense of power by shaming the men whose wives he pursued, men who had a position in society such as wealthy merchants, landlords and babus working with the British East India Company. Cuckolding was an act of hostility carried out by one man against another, using the latter's wife as a pawn. This illuminated the extent to which Bukka was willing to go, by exploiting and derailing the bond between a husband and wife for his own satisfaction. To Bukka cuckolding gave him power over other men and their wives. In the absence of any emotional attachment Bukka exploited these wife turned mistresses to make their husbands jealous and cause their husbands mental anguish. He knew that the men whose wives, sisters and mistresses he sought were all too aware that, if they were cuckoled they would stand to loose their honour and this offered Bukka the perfect scheme for gaining power over the husbands by insulting the honour of their wives. To find such married, neglected wives of prominent men who wanted to get away from their unfit husbands who drank all day long and were addicted to smoking marijuana, Bukka utilised the services of women like Bullemma who acted as a finder, facilitator and procureress. These wives became mistresses because they questioned the necessity for them to stay at home especially when their menfolk were with prostitutes. The wives of such men, still in their youth and looking for someone to love in the form of a lover or a surrogate husband invariably fell into the trap set by the procureress, if they were dim witted or too naive to understand what they were getting into. In due course of time, the wife turned mistress learnt how to please her rich lover by using her eyes, speaking sweetly, pretending to be shy, walking in a provocative manner, dancing, hiding the names of other paramours, fooling and beguiling a big client through tricks and coquetry, if he came to know about the other paramours and ensuring that she gets paid for her services beforehand. The relationship between Bukka and the wife turned mistresses was a parasitic relationship where he exploited them as long as their youth and beauty lasted and they inturn exploited him for as long as the money in his pocket lasted and was able to provide them with a lavish lifestyle.

In some other cases wives became mistresses with the knowledge of their impotent husbands who allowed themselves to be cuckolded, so that their wife could bear children to continue with the family name even if it meant allowing a secret lover to visit her at home. Strangely enough the desire for children was so strong that it overrode any concern for the relationship with the wife and so long as the husband's name and reputation remained protected, the husband accepted his cuckolding with equanimity. The concern of a husband for his wife who did not return home on most nights was superficial and his wife's desire to pursue a sexual relationship with another man did not prompt the husband to re-evaluate his relationship with his wife and make any effort to mend it. This lack of ethical values on the part of the husband, at times, inflamed the wife with a similar passion and led her to cast off her own morals and inhibitions. However after the birth of one or two children this method which came into existance because of the need to beget children, came to a dead end with the impotent husband accepting the children as his own. This however did not prevent the wife's lover or lovers from visiting her and engaging in sex without impregnating her. The husband likewise had his own lovers about whom the wife knew, a perfect example of a polyamorous relationship in which the husband and wife had one or more sexual partners with mutual consent. A polyamorous relationship is a type of non-monogamous relationship in which multiple people are involved, characterised by a primary couple that openly (and with mutual consent) engage with other romantic partners." The fundamental philosophy of polyamory is that sexual love should not be confined to the strictures of monogamy but expressed freely and fully, another tenant of polyamory is that both individuals know of their partner's lovers". Zamindars like Shankar Dev Rao, his second son Bukka Dev Rao and their mistresses enjoyed being in a polyamorous relationships with a number of similar couples (while protecting their own womenfolk including their wives and daughters by keeping them in zanana ie behind a veiled purda).The zamindar and his son at times impregnated the women with whom they were in this kind of a relationship and this often led to unwanted pregnancies and the proliferation of their progeny in very many villages.

It was during this time ie during the period of Baji Rao Peshwa-I, polyamory took a bizarre turn when a game called Ghat Kanchuki which was played in Pune became a rage. Within a short period of time this game became a hot favourite with a large section of the zamindars in India. Both Bukka and Rudra actively participated in the game which was held in different secret locations from time to time. The game involved an equal number of men and women, generally around 8 men and 8 women ie 8 couples, who assembled at a secret location at night. This was done without any consideration to the caste or the relationship to one another. The group sat in a circle on a mattress with a chakra or a wheel drawn in the middle. All the members of the group knew one another. Then the women removed their clothes and after disrobing completely, put their clothes into a pot which was placed at the centter of the chakra. Each man in the group picked a cloth at random from the pot, (taken off by one of the women) thereby selecting his female partner for the night. The game continued till every one of those present had slept with a randomly selected partner. Then another secret location and date was chosen by the group and its new incumbents to continue the game. In accordance with ancient Tantric texts and keeping in mind the cardinal rule that whatever happened on the night the game was played, would not be discussed or disclosed to anyone.

This apart the zamindar, his son Bukka and Rudra had entered into sham marriages with any number of women.

The concept of a sham marriage was already in vogue and to enact a sham marriage the would be courtesan's mother selected a suitable paramour, someone like Bukka or Rudra for her daughter after she attained puberty, she ie the would be courtesan had, as a rule, to go through a form of marriage with a young man.

There was a very clever way of increasing the market value of one to be initiated into prostitution. The mother got together a lot of young men of the same age, nature and knowledge as her daughter and told them that she would give her daughter in marriage to the person who was in a position give her presents of a particular kind and value. After this the mother gave her daughter in marriage to the man who was ready to give her daughter the presents agreed upon. The girl ie the daughter could select her own husband but the consent of her mother was necessary. There was a great demand for the privilege of deflowering a virgin and heavy demands were made on the purse of the would be first paramour or so called husband. The would be first paramour or so called husband, before the marriage, gave a large sum in advance towards the expenses likely to be incurred in the ceremony.

After performing some sort of ceremony the first paramour was called the husband of the girl. The temporary bond lasted for a year. Thereafter the girl was free to prostitute herself. Her first paramour was responsible for maintaining her for at least a year, after which he was no longer bound by the bonds of marriage.

Thus the zamindar ie Shankar Dev Rao, Bukka and Rudra enjoyed the virginity of very many young women without entailing any legal obligation, as a result of such an ingenious marriage. However at times when a suitable man was not available, the wedding or the nuptial was symbolically done or contracted with a stick, a sword, a knife, a tree or an idol in place of the first paramour or so called husband so as to introduce the daughter into the business of concubinage or prostitution.

"A society dominated by men who sequestered their wives and daughters, denigrate the female role in reproduction, erect monuments to the male genetalia, have sex with the sons of their peers, sponsor public whorehouses, create a mythology of rape and engage in rampant sabre rattling", was what Athens was in medieval times as described in Eva.C. Keuls book 'The Reign of the Phallus: Sexual Politics in Ancient Athens. Unfortunately, very unfortunately the system in most parts of India under nawabs, rajas and zamindars from the 16th to the end of the 19th century AD was no different.

Chapter 16

The Departed

After failing miserably in all his efforts to ferret out his father's killers Bukka realised that it was beyond him. He reconciled with the death of his father and went back to his old ways which included stripping naked and diving into a village pond in which women folk were bathing on one side. Bukka like his father was a very strong man, he had learnt to use weapons and was a formidable fighter and he was also a good marksman. Bukka had the kind of body that women craved for and he did not make any effort to hide his body which he flaunted at any and every opportunity that presented itself. On this particular occasion on a hot and sultry moonlit night, Bukka went to the pond which was within the zamindar's estate and which his late father was in the habit of frequenting. Slowly Bukka removed his clothes and slid into the cool waters of the pond, he was a very good swimmer and after swimming a couple of laps he came to one corner of the pond and took out a bottle of liquor and had just started to drink when a movement in the undergrowth drew his attention. Bukka picked up his dagger and slowly made his way to a clearing in the undergrowth in which something which gave an awful stench was lying in the middle. Very, very slowly Bukka approached whatever was on the ground, but in the dim moon light he could not make out what it was. Under the circumstances he withdrew from the thicket and went back to the mansion where he called his guards and accompanied by his guards he went back to the thicket and retrieved whatever was lying on the ground. Back in the mansion and in as much light as was available, his guards opened the cloth blanket that held whatever they had picked up, then they fell on their knees when they realised that what they were seeing was what was left of the zamindar of Mahadevpalli, skin, bones, teeth and hair ie skull and bones. They could positively identify him because of the gold rings and gold chains that the late zamindar was in the habit of wearing. Bukka wept as he had not wept for anyone, his father was very dear to him, while cursing God and mankind for what had happened to his father.

Bukka despite being the younger son of the zamindar was closer to him. He was similar to his father in his attitude towards women, in his contempt for his fellow human beings, in his desire to satisfy himself at all costs and desire to possess that which did not belong to him including the wives of other men once he laid his eyes on them. He was a person who brooded on the world around him and disliked what he saw. He could be brilliant at times, depressive at other times with just one constant in his life, he was a man who was increasingly isolated at all times. A man who did not trust or love anyone barring his father, a person who even entertained the vile idea that his elder brother Vikram Dev Rao may have been involved with his father's death with the hope of usurping the family wealth and the diamonds that his late father had acquired, but with the discovery of his father's remains and the fact that Vikram Dev Rao was away in Pune for over 6 months (was nowhere in the picture and it would take over a month for him to return) put an end to Bukka's pet idea of linking his father's death with Vikram in any way.

That very night Bukka and the other family members cremated the remains of the zamindar and swore everyone who was present to silence. The next morning Bukka, his son and a large number of their staff and guards thoroughly searched the undergrowth and the thicket where Bukka found the mortal remains of his father but nothing came out of the search. Thereafter Bukka began to drink even during the day, something was troubling him, something that he was unable to come to terms with. Bukka was spending more time at home and on many an occasion he did not leave the house even with his guards after darkness had fallen. Bukka was missing his nocturnal activity and the sexual escapades that followed, he was in an irritable frame of mind and as evening turned to night and night to late night his irritability peaked.

On this occasion after a month of literally hiding like a hermit crab, Bukka Dev Rao stood on the balcony with a glass of liquor in his hand looking at the setting Sun, when down below the side entrance to the house opened and Bullemma the wife of the cattle grazer and the younger sister of Chellamma the wife of the cook

Mallanna who worked as a maid, came out. Bullemma was young, good looking, voluptuous or you may say chubby, with a raunchy sex appeal. She had come out to see if Bukka was on the terrace, on seeing him she smiled and quietly made her way to a section of the house where hay was stacked, a hayshed, where hay was kept to feed the cattle, which included cows, buffaloes and the Zamindar's bulls.

Her association with Bukka was like a butterfly that fluttered for a day and thought it is forever, just as the power she exercised was the result of catering to Bukka's vanity, who was like a cock which thought that the sun had risen to hear him crow. Bullemma was aware that Bukka was devoured by a terrible ambition and that was to please himself at all costs, the only handicap was that he was born, living and forever lazy. If ever there was anything that moved Bukka it was fear of the unknown and self interest. She also knew that Bukka's half brother Vikram Dev Rao was also driven by self interest but unlike Bukka he was not blind, he was sharp sighted. Bullemma in her own eyes was not actually sleeping with Bukka, in her mind she was sleeping with the abstract concept of tremendous money, power and position. It was not as if Bukka was exploiting her for sex, she was also exploiting his weakness for her, it was a symbiotic relationship in which each utilised the other.

On spotting her Bukka went into the house, lit an oil fired lamp and casually sauntered across to the cattle shed and then to the room where the hay was stacked.

As soon as he entered he heard a low whisper "I am over here", Bukka climbed up a ladder to a loft above the hay stack using the lamplight to guide him. Bullemma was lying on the hay waiting for him with a desperate, passionate, yearning look in her eyes which left no room for any doubt. Bukka placed the lamp on one side carefully to make sure it does not tilt and to ensure that the hay did not catch fire. Then he concentrated on Bullemma, he took off her blouse revealing her well rounded, tight breasts with dark nipples, he found her breasts mesmerising. He fondled them while kissing her passionately on her lips and neck, he kissed her until she was breathless and clung to him, then he moved down to her breasts and her protruding nipples and kneaded her breasts. He caressed her naked stomach and thighs with his hands and mouth. The intense and absolutely sensual noises of pleasure she made as he plundered her with his tongue inflamed his raw passion. He eased her legs apart, settled himself within the cradle of her thighs and sank into her in one fluid motion. He embedded himself between the stretching walls of her body, she gasped and lifted herself up with her hands around his neck and kissed him. He delved deeper into her with each rhythmic thrust. After a while he stopped thrusting, her moans had turned into a long high-pitched orgasm. Bullemma wrapped her legs tightly around Bukka's waist and pulled him closer, they shared one last passionate kiss before settling into a blissful state of post-coital afterglow. She loved to talk dirty especially after sex, at times she was downright crude but Bukka did not find it disorienting, he just thought she was absolutely hot, to him her vulgarity was like garlic in the salad of taste, he caressed her. Then Bukka rolled off and lay on one side on his elbow, stroking Bullemma's breasts with one hand and then gently sliding his hand over her stomach down to her navel, Bullemma's body quivered like a woman in the throes of deep passion. As he touched her intimately, she did the same to him, she raked her hands and fingers over his chest, she caressed his face and her gaze along with various non-verbal cues conveyed that she was both emotionally and sexually aroused.

After a while Bullemma's breathing which was labored became normal and she said "do you know Kishtiah the kirana shop owner and Yellamma's daughter Kumi who live in Nagepalli, is getting married to Vamsi the son of Purniah and Lalitamma who run a small kirana shop in Sompalli". Bukka said "is that so, you keep an eye on them, as soon as the wedding is over let me know". Bullema said with a mischievous smile "you want to have your fill of her before her husband deflowers her, she is a real beauty", Bukka laughed to him sex relieved tension where as love caused it, he did not love anyone, sex was the consolation because he could not love anyone or be loved by anyone and planted one last passionate kiss on Bullema's lips, wore his dothi and taking the oil lamp quietly got down from the loft and made his way back to his own bedroom in the mansion.

About a month later Bullemma informed Bukka that the wedding of Vamsi and Kumi was scheduled at 4 o' clock the following day, the two of them would spend the night at Kumi's place and leave for Vamsi's house the following day. Bukka bided his time then at around 8 o' clock at night he sent his men to fetch Kumi. Both Vamsi and Kumi had bathed and were about to have their dinner when Bukka's men arrived and quietly informed Kumi's parents that the zamindar's horse drawn carriage was waiting for her. There was no resistance except from Kumi who looked at her parents and her husband to prevent Bukka's men from taking her, but he had taken care of that. Bukka had sent a zari sari and a gold sovereign as a gift, it had the added effect of silencing Kumi's parents and her husband. Kumi was taken to Bukka's bed room where he informed her that from now onwards he was her protector and benefactor. Kumi had every reason to despise her husband after he had literally sold her. On the other hand she had no reason to disbelieve Bukka's words that he was her benefactor and protector, given the fact that apart from his wealth, he was strong, handsome and manly in comparison to her husband who was short, dark and emaciated (heavy drinking had taken a toll of his body). Bukka gently picked Kumi up in his arms and placed her on his bed and made passionate love to her. In that short period of time while making a weak attempt to fend off Bukka's amorous love making, Kumi discovered more about her own unexplored deepest and darkest sexual fantasies, pressure points in her body that gave her an orgasm and the nuances of sensual love making than she could have imagined with her spineless husband Vamsi in all the days to come, for whom the gold coin was of greater importance than Kumi. In Vamsi's calculation Kumi was always there but a gold coin which in those days was a very large sum of money was not easy to comeby. Later on that night Kumi was sent back to her husband where life went on as usual. Bukka had deflowered dozens of virgins on their nuptial night, but there was hardly a whisper of dissent fom anyone, this pernicious system was accepted by the villagers in all the villages around Mahadevpalli as a necessary evil right from the day the zamindar Shankar Dev Rao, a vassal of the Marathi chieftain Shivaji had established himself in Mahadevpalli.

All this went on while Bukka's own wife churned and fretted with humiliation in one of the neighbouring rooms, while her husband on many an occasion enjoyed sex with young and luscious virgins on their marital night, prior to returning them to their husbands. Parvathi Devi knew that she was nothing more than a piece of prized but used furniture to whom he turned once in a blue moon. At all other times, she had to live with memories of making love to Bukka, in those days when she was young and nubile with a fresh and buxom body. Parvathi Devi loved Bukka despite all his wrong doings, to which, she feigned blindness on any number of occasions. To her Bukka was her husband, nothing else mattered. By and large, with exceptions, marriage was itself a lopsided affair, married women were not expected to get any pleasure or enjoyment from their marital status, they simply got married to abide by the moral/ social code and to procreate. Subservient wives who did not entertain any idea of becoming a married mistress to someone else were expected to turn a blind eye to their husband's infidelity. Men however were allowed to sleep around as much as they liked with anyone they chose. In this context prostitutes, dancing girls, mistresses and slaves were considered fair game.

On the other hand, Parvathi could not expect an iota of sympathy or even a word of support from her son who was more voyeuristic than his father. Infact it was rumoured that Rudra had already surpassed his father's record of deflowering young women. Their infamous sexual exploits were so famous that both father and son were the subject of gossip not only in the ninety villages which came under the zamindar of Mahadevpalli but also in other far off places. The only person she could turn to was her sister-in-law Maheshwari Devi the wife of Vikram Dev Rao, the elder son of the zamindar. Both of them and their two children Surya Dev Rao and Lakshmi Devi were the only people whom Parvathi Devi felt were decent and deeply religious, apart from her mother in law Yamini Devi. But all this had changed, after she planted the small bird's egg shaped blood ruby like seed. Now she was perfectly at home, alone by herself with the vine growing outside her window. She was no longer in need of anyone to turn to, she had a new companion.

After another month or so Bukka felt confident, there was no reason for him to fear anyone, because after the brutal treatment that he meted out to a lot of people subsequent to his father's death, he was feared and he knew that they feared him. His erractic ways and his unconventional way of thinking out of the box, coupled with his distrust of any and every one made him "an untouchable, an enfant terrible". He sent word to Bullemma to await his arrival in the hayshed. After darkness fell, Bukka went to the hayshed with an oil lamp to light up the way. On his arrival and after climbing up the loft where she waited for him he did not find her. Bukka drew his sword, he sensed danger was at very close quarters, then he heard Bullemma weeping form somewhere deeper inside the hayshed. Bukka went to look for her, the hay had been displaced towards the rear portion of the hayshed, indicating that a violent struggle had taken place. In the dim lamp light he saw Bullemma's clothes lying scattered on the hay. The sound of weeping came from the rear of the hayshed which had a door. The door was ajar and Bukka thought that whoever had molested Bullemma had dumped her outside the rear door. Beyond the rear door was an open space and beyond the open space was thick undergrowth. No one came to this part of the estate. Bukka slowly made his way out of the rear door and lifted the lamp so as to cast the light on a larger area. At that very moment he distinctly heard his late father calling out to him "Bukka I am here, come to me". Bukka was confused and he replied "where are you nana?", the reply came immediately "right in front of you my son". Before Bukka could overcome his confusion and look around, something knocked the lamp out of his hands extinguishing the lamp light. In the moonlight very strong creeper/vine like appendages wrapped themselves around Bukka and given the fact that he was in a highly inebriated state of mind, since he had been drinking throughout the evening, his normally razor sharp reflexes were numbed and within a short period of time hundreds of tiny suckers entered deep into his skin and devoured him. In his dying moments Bukka knew what had happened to his late father but it was too late, his chapter was over.

After Bukka failed to return that night, Yamini Devi ordered that each and every corner of the house should be searched. Someone mentioned that they had seen Bullemma enter the hayshed and that after a while Bukka too entered the same hayshed. Yammini Devi asked the guards assisted by a large number of staff members to thoroughly search the hayshed and the area beyond the hayshed including the undergrowth in the early hours of the morning. She had no faith in late night searches which had not yielded any results earlier on. Early the next morning the search began and after a short while they located the decrepit remains of Bullemma's body. A deeper search produced Bukka's body in the same state. That very day the mortal remains of Bukka were cremated in accordance with Vedic rituals accompanied by the recital of a number of mantras.

Apart from Rudra, who was paralysed with fear, there were only women folk in the house. Parvathi Devi was strangely enough not only composed but she did not appear to be highly perturbed. Her behaviour however went unnoticed in the light of the two strange developments that had taken place in a short span of time. The first development was the strange manner in which the zamindar's body surfaced after disappearing, the second development was that of Bukka's and Bullemma's death in the hands of some very murky, sinister and unknown predator. The entire household awaited the return of Vikram Dev Rao from Pune.

Chapter 17

Vikram Dev Rao returns

Prior to Vikram Dev Rao's return the whole house was washed clean and a number of holy men were invited by Yamini Devi to do poojas, recite mantras and to purify the house. The idea was to get rid of any unholy or evil spirit. A few days after his return, Vikram Dev Rao took stock of the situation and after attending to the day's engagement, finally found some leisurely time to be with his wife. He observed her for some time and then choosing his words carefully he said "Maheshwari you are looking tired, the last few months have been very very unusual". Maheshwari said "yes, Lakshmi had come to be with me, she went back to Rajanpalli only a couple of days back, amma (Yamini Devi) has not come out of the shock, she calls me to be with her before going to sleep every night. I stay with her until she goes to sleep. As for as Parvathi is concerned, she has become very very silent, since the zamindar's body surfaced mysteriously and after the death of Bukka and Bullemma in one night under very mysterious circumstances. The cattle grazer goes around like he has been slapped by a ghost, he was not very fond of Bullemma but she was after all his wife and the way she died like Bukka, has unnerved him and a lot of other people who stay on the estate".

Vikram Dev Rao watched his wife Maheshwari while she removed her gold bangles, heavy gold chains and wear a simple cotton saree and blouse, after taking a bath, before going to sleep. His love for her was just as strong as on the day he saw her for the first time, she was beautiful and vivacious, it had not turned into a love affair with a beginning and an end as was the case with many married couples, it was only love between the two of them. He knew she had gone through a lot in the months he was away and was the only person his mother Yamini Devi could turn to, in the days preceding and after the death of his father and Bukka. Vikram said "I have been away for a considerable period of time and it was not possible for me to talk to you at length, I know what all happened, but still I want to know from you, what was it like when I was not around?". Maheshwari replied "it was eerie and peculiarly silent after nana (the zamiṇdar Shankar Dev Rao) died, even more frightening after his body disappeared", then Vikram asked her "what was Bukka's reaction?" Maheshwari replied "he was totally devastated on one hand, on the other hand his anger was grim and palpable because he felt that someone had done it on purpose". Then Vikram asked Maheshwari "what was your reaction and how did Parvathi Devi take it?" Maheshwari said "I was confused and frightened, Parvathi Devi was strangely very silent, and it was as if she was not in this world". Then Maheshwari said "I had asked Lakshmi to come and be with me, the two of us spent our time indoors and mostly with amma (Yamini Devi)".

She extinguished the lamp and apart from the moonlight that filtered into the room through the open window there was no other light. Maheshwari lay on the bed next to Vikram, in the darkness he snuggled up to his wife. She was aware that he had been watching her. She rolled over and came closer to him. The long period of separation aroused his passion and he embraced her lovingly. He slowly removed her clothes and covered her naked body with kisses until she trembled with delight. To him her taste, her smell and her feel so close to him left time and space with no meaning, it was only his overwhelming desire for her. He kissed her passionately on her mouth while fondling her teardrop breasts and nipples. He leaned down pressing his mouth between her luscious breasts, then he pinned her tightly to the bed, she reacted with more audible moans. He grabbed her hips and shafted her sex, her resisting flesh split and he slid completely into her passion moistened depths. She gasped and groaned and brought her knees up to accommodate him, her body shuddered as ripples of orgasmic ecstasy flooded her. Her arousal gushed through her like a tidal wave against which she was helpless. She grabbed his hair and dragged him down, pressing all her soft lush curves against his body, he held her tenderly and kissed her with untamed desire. After fully venting their passion, they collapsed in each other's arms. Maheshwari used a towel to wipe herself and fell deep asleep, sex and loving had left her feeling on top of the world but at the same time she was very exhausted, afterall she was not in her youth, she was the mother of a son and a married daughter.

Maheshwari was feeling much better after her husband's return. His return had restored her self confidence to a great extent. To be frank she was shaken with the way her father-in-law, her husband's half brother and the cattlegrazer's wife had died.

A few weeks later a strange incident took place. It had rained and a bolt of lightening fell on a mango tree burning it to the ground. This was considered to be very inauspicious and Maheshwari Devi felt that apart from cleansing the house by doing various poojas, a pilgrimage to the Mahanandi temple and Ahobilam, would go a long way in restoring the feeling that "all is well" since the entire household was on tenterhooks because of all the bizarre and inexplainable incidents that had taken place of recent. Under the circumstances the suggestion put forth by Maheshwari Devi that the family should undertake a pilgrimage to the Mahanandi temple and Ahobilam was readily accepted. Rudra stayed back to take care of the property, his mother Parvathi Devi said she was unwell and that she could not undertake such a long journey.

The road to the Mahanandi temple led through dense forests, the temple was located in the midst of dense forests, dating back to over 1500 years and consisting of nine Nandi shrines. The inscriptions on tablets from the 10th century speak of the temple being repaired and reconstructed several times. Mahanandi, Shivanandi, Vinayakanandi, Somanandi, Prathamanandi, Garudanandi, Suryanandi, Krishna nandi (also known as Vishnunandi) and Naganandi are the nine temples.

The Mahanandi Temple is renowned for its pools of fresh water, called Kalyani or Pushkarini. The temple's architecture demonstrates the strong presence of the Chalukya Kings in this region. The pools at the Mahanandi temple near *Nandyal*, demonstrate the ability of the Vishwakarmas. Three pools surround the main temple, two small pools at the entrance and one large pool inside the temple itself.

With an outdoor pavilion called a mandapa in the centre, this holy tank was about 60 square feet. The tank inlets and outlets are arranged in such a way that the water depth is constantly kept at five feet, allowing pilgrims to bathe in the holy water. Bathing in the large pool inside is forbidden every day after 5 pm.

A distinctive feature of the source of water here is that it is perennial.The water appears to originate below the Swayambhu Linga in the Garbhagriha (inner shrine). The water is tepid and is known for its healing qualities and in those days pilgrims invariably found gold specks, gold dust and a lucky few even found gold nuggets carried by the water from gold bearing rock stratas in the heavily forested area around the temple.

(Gold deposits in Rayalaseema: Rayalaseema is literally a gold mine! The region has a huge potential for gold mining and is the only region in India where two exclusive gold mines are being set up by an Australian-Indian organisation. There are known deposits of gold bearing quartz rocks in the Rayalaseema region which includes areas in Anantapur, Chittoor and Kurnool. The Mahanandi temple is close to the gold bearing areas in Kurnool).

The wildlife, especially tigers, leopards and black panthers, was so abundant that all the pilgrims to the temple stayed within the fortress like wall surrounding the temple, with the interior areas of the temple lit by burning brands of wood at night. After staying two full days in Mahanandi, the entire family moved towards a village enroute to Ahobilam. The distance of about 80 kms was covered by bullock carts in a single day. Night was spent in the village and early in the morning, on the following day the last stretch of the journey was completed on foot.

Ahobilam: There are nine Narasimha temples around the Nallamala forest range and in terms of sculpture and architecture all the nine temples stand as an ultimate testament to the ancient sthapathis who planned and sculpted these temples.

According to the legend, when the Devas saw the manifestation of Lord Vishnu as half-man (nara), half-lion(simha), they shouted "Ahobala" (great strength) as well as "Ahobila" (great cave in which the current sanctum is). Hence, the place can be called "Ahobalam" or "Ahobilam". This place is mentioned in the Brahmanda Purana. The place where Lord Narayana ie Narasimha swamy appeared from the stone pillar to kill Hiranyakashipa can be seen in this place. The name of this pillar is Ugra Sthambha or "Ukku Sthambha" in Telugu. After slaying Hiranyakasipa, Lord Narsimha swamy roamed around the forested hills of Ahobilam making fearsome sounds, before settling down at nine locations to bless the devotees called the Nava Narasimha temples. According to another legend Lord Garuda did penance to see Lord Vishnu in the form of Lord Narasimha. For this purpose Lord Narasimha took nine different forms in this hill. The nine forms of Lord Narasimha are: Bhargava Narasimha Swamy, Yogananda Narasimha Swamy, Chatravata Narasimha Swamy, Ahobila (Ugra) Narasimha Swamy (This is the main form of Lord Narasimha and is also referred as the main temple in Upper Ahobilam), Varaha Narasimha Swamy, Malola Narasimha Swamy, Jwala Narasimha Swamy, Paavana Narasimha Swamy, Karanja Narasimha Swamy.

The return from Ahobilam was uneventful and for sometime thereafter, there was no unnatural incident on the zamindar's estate in Mahadevpalli.

Chapter 18

Diwali

After the death of his father and his grand father, Rudra Dev Rao went around with a haunted look, the look of a condemned man. He was no different from both his grandfather and his father, he enjoyed what they enjoyed which was the company of multiple women and inflicting pain on his fellow human beings. This similarity was the very reason for his fear because whatever it was that had hunted down his father and his grandfather had a way of choosing the victims, strangely enough they all had the same character or lack of character and other low down qualities which made them and him stand apart. Rudra was not a fearless tiger like his father, he was more of a nocturnal leopard. Bukka could fight in the open but Rudra was cunning and depended on his guile to ambush his opponents and kill them. He did not take the death of his grandfather and his father lightly. He knew he was up against a very shadowy, formidable opponent who did not strike in broad daylight, someone or some thing that bided its time and struck at the opportune moment, when the victim was incapacitated or unable to react as fast as they would have reacted, under normal circumstances.

Rudra started spending time away from Mahadevpalli. He would spend time with a beautiful Anglo Indian woman who had come to him for help and ended up becoming his mistress in Madanapalli. The reason for this shift was not because he was very fond of her, but because he did not want to be anywhere close to Mahadevpalli, until he had time to think rationally about what had happened and decide on what measures he should take for his own survival, which for some unexplainable reason he felt was at risk. In the meantime, he got a regular feedback from Maya about day to day activities in the zamindar's estate in Mahadevpalli. Rudra spent time on his favourite sport "cockfighting". Cockfighting was not just a sport but it was also a big money spinner, a lot of zamindars were engaged in this sport and actively betted huge sum of money on their cocks. For Rudra winning was just as important, as it was to see his opponent's cock dying of injuries inflicted during the fight when special breeds of cocks were pitted in mortal combat against one another.

Cockfighting

The well-heeled, full-feathered battle cock was indeed a feathered warrior by extension. The owner and the handler of the battle ready cock placed themselves in the arena. The extension of man as the battle cock is of supreme importance when looking at the mystique of cockfighting. Cockfighting is a very male-oriented sport. The term cock itself is a common reference to the male genitals. "Cocky" is a term that means proud and boastful which Rudra was. The fighting cock is absolutely without fear, even when mortally wounded and in severe shock, the cock will continue to fight, an attribute that Rudra greatly admired. This apart, the primal urge of the hunter killer was also satisfied when Rudra pitted his battle cock armed with sharp blades tied to its talons or a sharp spike tied to its feet, against another cock.

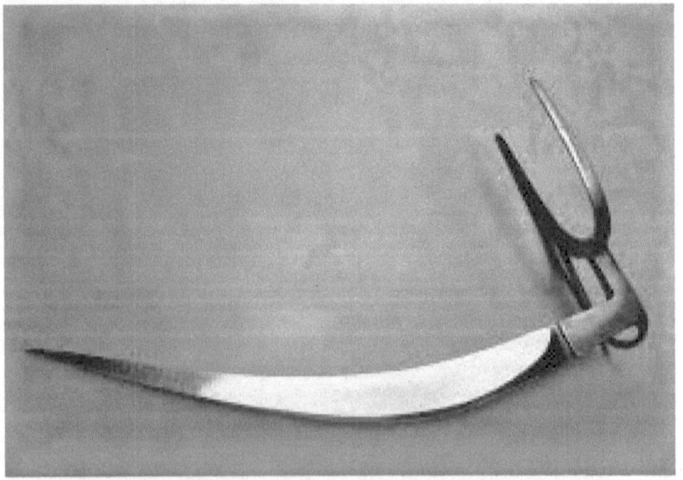

A sharp spike that was tied to the cock's feet

The cock not only fought for him ie the master, but fought to the death. In order to win the battle the cock must kill his opponent. Every aggressive urge that is supressed in a civil society was given a free run for a few moments while the fight between the cocks went on. To see a demonstration of this all one has to do is watch the reaction of the crowd as favorites win or die. Most leave a cockfight as emotionally and physically spent, as if they had engaged in extreme sexual activity. The release is not sexual but the physical and emotional release is very similar. The adrenalin flows in the spectators and participants, produced a high, that neither drugs nor alcohol could duplicate. A cockfight was from ancient times a single sex activity controlled by males with only male participants, very few women showed any intrest in it. In the cockpit all societal positions were forgotten and all the money in the world was of no use, when a cock died under the spurs of his opponent. Rudra and his fellow cockers were drawn from a broad segment of society, but in the 18th century they constituted a very close knit group.

A month or so later Rudra came back to the mansion in Mahadevpalli, but he confined himself to his room especially after darkness fell. To further ensure his safety, two of his most trusted body guards slept on the floor in his bedroom and he refrained from going out to visit anyone after sunset. Even Maya came to his room in the mansion during daylight hours to see him. Rudra lived the life of a hunted animal for almost three months until one day he overcame the fear and decided to live life to the brim once again.

Rudra Dev Rao was a spitting image of his father when it came to having sex, everything in Rudra's world was about sex except sex. Sex was about power. He had a longing for Maya the petite and very good looking elder daughter of Satyaraju and his wife, both of whom worked as servants in the zamindar's house. Maya was tall and fair with a slim and beautiful body which Rudra wanted to ravish, he had to have her, she oozed sex. Maya lived with her parents in a small house which was allotted by the zamindar to them located on the estate, so that they could be close at hand to attend to any work that was assigned to them at any time of the day or night. Rudra cleverly arranged to meet Maya in her own house after he gave her parents some work, which entailed travelling to the neighbouring village and returning to Mahadevpalli the next day in the morning before lunch. That night Rudra waited for nightfall and then went to the rear portion of Maya's house and knocked on the rear door. It was opened immediately, she was waiting for him. Rudra hugged Maya and planted tiny, tender kisses on her lips, she kissed him back with equal passion, then he kissed her on her neck and removed her sari and blouse and pushed her down on a thick mattress on the floor, he spread her legs wide, the secret of her feminity lay bare in front of him, she closed her eyes. He kissed her beautiful slender breasts and pert nipples until he could no longer resist her increasing passion. She felt alive in his hands, he caressed her nipples, cupped her breasts in his palms and gently fondled them. She moved closer to him, he plunged deep into her, entering her over and over again, she raised her hips in surrender to wave after wave of pleasure, instinctively wrapping her legs around him and driving him even deeper. She moaned a sound which she did not know she was capable of, it was relief, gratitude and yearning for more and it created an even more intimate heat that ignited the brisk night, transforming their liaison into a heavenly experience. She was seized by a rush of sensation so intense that she could not hold back a scream of pleasure, the immensity was compounded when she felt spasms of his release deep inside her. He buried his face in the perfumed cloud of her hair spread on the mattress as intense pleasure surged through their bodies. They continued to make love rolling around on the tattered mattress in various positions, making each touch and affectionate gesture count, her bite marks were like love notes written on his flesh, then they lay back on the mattress and cherished the feeling.

Later on that night Rudra got up after tenderly caressing Maya's body in the darkness and said "I am not afraid of anyone, but you be careful. I do not want to loose you". Maya said "Rudra please do not go anywhere without your bodyguards, this place is beginning to frighten me, I am unable to sleep, I feel we are being watched". Rudra said "I am certain I heard my father calling me by my name but when I came out, there was nobody", Maya said "very strange, I also heard Bullemma calling out to her husband, I waited for a while, nothing happened so I thought that I must have been dreaming". Rudra said "God knows what is happening, come sit here, I want you close to me ". Maya was among the few women who inspired tenderness after sex and Rudra was among those few men who did not fake it. Maya said "when I am with you, we stay up all night but when you are not there, I cannot go to sleep". Rudra sat silently for a while then he quietly left Maya's house, she kissed him passionately on his lips which he reciprocated before she shut and bolted the heavy wooden door.

Diwali celebration in the zamindar's mansion was a muted affair for family members because of all the deaths. But Vikram Dev Rao had personally instructed those who worked in the mansion and those who worked on the zamindar's vast estate around the mansion to celebrate Diwali with fervour along with villagers from the nearby villages. The idea was to break the gloom and silence, that had come to become a part of their life and to usher in a new era of hope and happiness. Since ancient times, Diwali has been celebrated with ritual oil baths, consumption of delicious sweets, wearing new clothes and ornaments.

Religious perspective: In 527 BC, a 72-year-old spiritual master died in the city of Pawa in Bihar. All he had was his robe, till he abandoned clothes altogether. Naked, he pursued his spiritual quest, confronting many a challenge. In the process he was "beaten with sticks" and outside a village he was met by a mob that asked him to "get away." When he meditated, they "cut his flesh, tore his hair and covered him with dust". But the man persevered and by the time he died, he won legions of disciples and even kingly respect. He was Vardhaman Mahavir, the 24th Tirthankar of the Jains and it was on Diwali day, many centuries ago that his mortal existence came to an end. Down the ages Diwali has endured as a festival of tremendous significance in India. Some see it as having evolved from an autumnal agrarian celebration, the festival marks the annual return of a time when "the granaries are full of corn, the tension of labour and anxiety about the harvest is over and thus there is a natural tendency to celebrate".

To orthodox Jains, though, this was not originally about mere rejoicing as a day that marks the attainment of moksha (salvation) by Mahavir, it was at first spent in silence, fasting and other austerities as was experienced by the 24th Tirthankar. Over time, though, more cheerful elements made their way into the Jain Diwali. With many Jains being prosperous merchants and purveyors of trade, they too welcomed the Goddess of wealth to their homes on this day, paving Lakshmi's way with light and decorative opulence.

According to Hindu tradition, on this day, the hero of the Ramayan ie Lord Ram finally returned to his country and ascended the throne after 14 years in exile having won a victory over his asura foe, Ravana. According to a story from the great Indian epic, the Mahabharat, it was on Diwali eve that Krishna slayed the arrogant Narakasura, liberating 16,000 women he had enslaved. Even the Mughals like Emperor Akbar and Jahangir ensured the Mughals celebrated Diwali in their courts, while visitors to Vijayanagar in the south noticed the innumerable number of lamps of oil which was kept burning day and night, on this festive occasion.

The advent of gunpowder, interestingly, made Diwali an event featuring more than just magnificient lights. In the second half of the 18th century, for instance, the celebrated Maratha general Mahadji Scindia wrote to his master, the Peshwa, about events in Kota in Rajasthan. "The Diwali festival," he noted, "was celebrated for 4 days in Kota when lakhs of lamps were lit and there was a fine display of fireworks in the capital".

In ancient India Diwali was seen as the festival when Lord Rama came back to Ayodhya, after killing the devil king Ravana, with his wife Goddess Sita and his younger brother Lakshman and his devotee Hanuman. People celebrated this day by lighting diyas at their home, making the whole of Ayodhya lit up. A festival of lights and a night of fireworks is enchanting. "The use of fireworks in the celebration of Diwali came into existence after about 1400 AD with the usage of gunpowder in warfare in India." Fireworks, like its primary ingredient gunpowder, have a long history in India.

Fireworks in medieval Indian celebration: One of the earliest observations was made by Abdur Razzaq, the ambassador of the Timurid Sultan Shahrukh to the court of the Vijayanagar king Devaraya II in 1443. Describing the events of the Mahanavami festival, Razzaq wrote, "One cannot without entering into great detail mention all the various kinds of pyrotechny and squibs and various other arrangements which were exhibited". Italian traveller Ludovico di Varthema who visited India in this period, made a similar observation while describing the city of Vijaynagar and its elephants: "But if at any time, they (elephants) are bent on flight, it is impossible to restrain them, for this race of people are great masters of making fireworks and these animals have a great dread of fire".

Fireworks and pyrotechnic shows existed as a form of royal entertainment in many medieval Indian kingdoms during festivals, events and special occasions like weddings. Manufacturing formulas for fireworks describing pyrotechnic mixtures are found within Kautukachintamani, a Sanskrit volume by Gajapati Prataparudradeva (1497-1539), a reputed royal author from Orissa.

It is notable that Ibrahim Adil Shah, the Sultan of Bijapur, circa 1609 AD gave a lavish dowry in the wedding of his courtier's daughter to the son of the Nizam Shahi general Malik Ambar, "with Rs. 80,000 being spent on fireworks alone". While rulers were primarily the organising sponsors of these shows, it is clear that other citizens also had access to fireworks. Duarte Barbosa, a writer and officer of Portuguese India who wrote some of the earliest pieces of travel literature, described a Brahmin wedding in Gujarat from his travels (circa 1518) where the bride and bridegroom "are entertained by the people with dancing and songs, firing of bombs and rockets in plenty, for their pleasure". His description, suggests that fireworks had been manufactured in India and were available in plenty in Gujarat at that time.

By the eighteenth century, fireworks on a grand scale became a part of Diwali entertainment organised by the rulers. Peshwayanchi Bakhar, a Maratha chronicle, mentions a recounted account of Diwali celebration in Kota. Mahadji Scindia in it describes to Peshwa Savai Madhavarao, "the Diwali festival is celebrated for 4 days at Kota", when lakhs of lamps are lit. The Raja of Kota during these 4 days gives a display of fire-works outside the premises of his capital. It is called "Lanka of fire-works". Mahadji then went on to describe an image of Ravana at the center, surrounded by rakshasas, monkeys and a big image of Hanuman, prepared in Gunpowder, which upon being lit actually illustrated the scene of Lanka dahan. After hearing this, the Peshwa gave orders for a similar display of fireworks for his entertainment. The resultant grand performance, as per the chronicle, was "witnessed by the people of Pune in large numbers".

The arrival of a skilled English pyrotechnician in India circa 1790 AD first impressed the British in Calcutta with his performance and was then sent by them to Asaf-ud-Daullah, the Nawab of Oudh, whom he regaled with a spectacular, continuous display in the sky of colorful fireflowers, fish, serpents and stars.

Thus, by the late Peshwa period, when the Mughal empire was breathing its last and the British East India

Company was realising its designs in India, not only was the knowledge of different fireworks common, but also many references to Diwali along with the accompanying description of fireworks or atishbazi began surfacing in various publications. Often these makers of fireworks were also the manufacturers of gunpowder, the raw materials for which was always readily available in India and which was used in warfare. By the end of the eighteenth century, however, its military use was phased out in favour of newer explosives like dynamite.

A few days after Diwali, Maya came to see Rudra, as soon as she entered his room, Rudra shut the massive teak wood doors and kissed her passionately. After a while Rudra asked Maya what was the reason for this sudden visit, Maya who was waiting for Rudra to ask this question said "Rudra you are going to be fabulously rich, the other day in broad daylight I went for a stroll around the mango orchard, I must have walked quite some distance when I noticed something lying on the ground. I looked closer and I found a small blood red ruby like seed, I looked around a little more carefully and I found that there was a mound of similar blood red ruby like seeds near a stunted tree. I collected whatever I could in a cloth bag". Rudra said with a look of great anticipation and greed in his eyes "Maya, did you bring the bag with you?" Maya said "yes, and produced a small cloth bag from beneath the folds of her saree, then she spilt the contents on Rudra's bed", Rudra could not believe his eyes, for all practical purposes the small egg shaped blood red seeds looked remarkably like rubies, nobody except for someone who knew the real story could have any reason to doubt that what was lying on Rudra's bed were not rubies. Rudra was ecstatic, he hugged Maya and planted many more kisses on her saying "baby we are going to be very rich", then he released her and sank on his bed. Maya lay beside him. Rudra asked Maya "did you tell anyone? Did anyone see you?" Maya replied "no, I did not tell anyone, not even my parents and no one saw me". Rudra said "Maya are you certain?" Maya replied "absolutely certain". Rudra said "Maya, I don't want anyone to know what you have discovered. We will collect as many of the small egg shaped blood red ruby like seeds and store it in a very safe place. We will get married and with the money we get from the sale of these ruby like seeds we can live life on our own terms either in Mahadevpalli or elsewhere". Maya rolled over and kissed Rudra. After sometime Rudra said to Maya "I want to go with you to see the exact spot where you saw these ruby like seeds. I will ask two of my most trusted guards to come with us, they have been with me from my childhood".

A short while later Maya, Rudra and his bodyguards quietly slipped out of the zamindar's mansion, unnoticed, from one of the side doors and on horse back slowly made their way to the location in the orchard, where a few days earlier Maya had found a heap of small blood red ruby like seeds. On reaching the location with Maya leading the way, Rudra found that there was a lot of blood red small egg shaped ruby like seeds strewn on the floor along with leaves and small mounds of similar seeds heaped near the base of the stunted trees at that location. Rudra was euphoric, he asked his guards to collect as many seeds as they could lay their hands on. What he and his guards collected with Maya giving a helping hand would fetch a fabulous sum of money, the kind of money that would elevate Rudra from a zamindar to a king. But Rudra was not satisfied. He wanted more and he made plans to come back later in the night, despite Maya's plea that coming out at night was dangerous. Rudra had lost his mind and in that euphoric condition his mind did not comprehend the danger that was lurking in the dark. Rudra said to Maya "my baby, this is once in a life time opportunity, if we do not take advantage of it someone else will, do you think Vikram Dev Rao and his son will let go and imagine our condition if they find this wealth, we will become beggars in our own house". Maya agreed, she was not happy but she agreed because Rudra was so adamant.

Later on that night after taking all precautions that they are not noticed Rudra, Maya and the two bodyguards quietly slipped out of the mansion once again on horse back, made their way to the spot in the orchard that they had visited earlier in the day. On reaching the spot Rudra got down to business and using lamp light for illumination he asked his guards to collect the small blood ruby like seeds. Then he told Maya that it was time to get back, at that moment something moved in the undergrowth and a very strong creeper/vine like appendage coiled itself around the feet of one of the body guards. Before the others could react many more vines coiled around the feet of Rudra and Maya and powerful suckers stung them before piercing their skin. In their last fear stricken moments Rudra, Maya and the body guards knew they had been tricked. This was a very cleverely laid out ploy which used Rudra's insatiable greed to draw him out into the open at night, what followed was what befell his father and his grand father.

The next day someone noticed horses roaming around in the orchard, someone from among those who saw the horses, recognized one of the horses as Rudra's horse. Vikram Dev Rao was informed and then a massive manhunt was launched. All that they found was sackfulls of the small blood red ruby like seeds. A search of Rudra's room revealed many more blood red ruby like seeds. However Rudra, Maya and his two bodyguards had disappeared without a trace.

Stuffed animals, hunting trophies

"Welcome to my nightmare, I think you're going to like it".

– Alice Coop

Chapter 19

The Darkness descends

Most of the household members and the staff had come to the conclusion that an evil spirit was responsible for the death of the zamindar, his son Bukka and the disappearance of his grandson Rudra. They also felt that whatever it was that was hunting select members of the zamindar's family was doing so with a vengeance ie to avenge something that was done in which these men had a very direct role to play. Most families who stayed on the estate decided to move into the main bungalow so that they could keep a closer watch on one another.

Pichiah and Kavita a young married couple lived in the zamindar's mansion and did all kinds of work that was given to them. It had been raining, Yamini Devi the wife of the zamindar had given them the day off because she was going to another village with a few family members to attend a wedding and to visit the temple of the Godess Sri Sivagami Sundari Amman.

Pichiah was starved for sex and once both of them got back to their room he warmed up to Kavita, then he took off her blouse so that he could gently caress and kiss her lovely well rounded breasts and nipples, she squealed with delight and was surprised to see that even without her active participation she was being turned on. Pichiah pushed Kavita down on a mat on the floor and removed her pavada, she gasped as he explored her naked body with both hands, felt the feminine curves of her hips. He was coaxing her body awake, stirring very deep sensual memories. She felt a throbbing ache between her thighs, her nipples tightened in response to his touch and she arched her back to push them into his hands, he groaned. She lay back invitingly with her legs parted, the damp petals of her womanhood exposed, "enter me" she whispered fervently and waited for the encroaching ecstasy. He positioned himself over her, kneeling between her knees and gently caressed her aching breasts, he leaned forward and guided his throbbing erection into her depths, she closed her eyes as a sharp surge of immense pleasure erupted from her core leading to a shuddering orgasm. He could no longer resist the increasing passion, her wriggling against him, her sighs and her legs pulling him deeper into her, with one last thrust he climaxed and exploded inside her. With their desire spent, she pushed him on the mat and and rested her head on his chest hearing his rapid heartbeat. He slid his hands down her back and playfully squeezed her buttocks, she let out a squeal of delight "Ooo..maa".

It had been a thoroughly rewarding night but they were afraid, there was something deeply wrong with the house. They had closed the windows and bolted the doors before settling down for the night but they kept one lamp burning, they were afraid of the darkness. Pichiah said in the semi darkness "I think we must leave this place and go to your parent's house in Sompalli for a few days". Kavita said "we will talk to Yamini Devi amma tomorrow morning. Go to sleep, it is very late." Pichiah, yawned and looked at his wife, lay down and was about to go to sleep when both of them heard a terrible crashing sound, as if a door or a window had been broken open or forced open. Then they heard footsteps, people were running for their life.

While Pichiah and Kavita were busy with one another just as darkness fell on this full moon night, in Vikram Dev Rao's room, Vikram, his wife Maheshwari and Parvathi Devi were discussing what all had happened in the last few months. Parvathi Devi was seated close to the open window when a cloud moved in front of the moon and in those couple of seconds Vikram and his Wife saw in the diffused moonlight very strong creeper/ vine like appendages that had grown at an astronomical pace outside their window, suddenly reach through the open window and wrap themselves around Parvathi Devi. She screamed in fear, but more creepers or the vine like appendages appeared and completely wrapped themselves around her. The grip on her flesh exerted through their suckers was tenacious. Vikram Dev Rao was the first to react, he took out his sword and slashed at the vines. But this did not break the grip that the vines had on Parvathi Devi's body, she had fainted out of sheer fear, before Vikram could take any other steps to protect Parvathi Devi, she was literally hoisted out of the open window and dragged deep into the mango orchard, away from any one's view. Vikram Dev Rao called for his body guards and went to look for Parvathi Devi after sending a few female members to attend to Maheshwari Devi who was hysterical. They searched for a long time in the moonlight and in the light cast by burning brands of wood that a vast majority of searchers carried but they could not locate Parvathi Devi's body.

After the search was called off, the usually inert creeper or vine like appendages which emerged from the stunted trees for the first time came alive not in a surrepticious or in a hidden manner, but in an open and brazen manner and wrapped themselves around a terror stricken farmhand and consumed him (this farmhand had participated in the tantric pooja and helped in sowing the small egg shaped blood ruby like seeds) in full view of another farmhand (both of whom had been working on the zamindar's estate and were returning late after smoking a tobacco leaf bidi) who tried to help, by using an axe to cut down a few vines. This angered the vines and they reacted by going on a blood thirsty rampage, attacking anything warm blooded that moved. All hell broke loose and a frightened crowd of people working on the zamindar's vast estate including his guards made a beeline for the zamindar's house and narrated what they saw to Vikram Dev Rao. He immediately instructed his guards to evacuate the women and children then he felt he would be free to take certain harsh steps to try and bring back normalcy.

Kavita immediately gathered a couple of clothes into a cloth bag, Pichiah had already opened the door. There was chaos outside, people were running helter skelter, when Pichiah heard Vikram Dev Rao's voice asking people to go towards the main entrance. Outside in the porch a dozen bullockcarts and guards on horseback were lined up, people were getting into the bullockcarts, then three or four very heavy chests belonging to Vikram Dev Rao was loaded into the carts and Maheshwari got into one of the carts, there was no sign of Parvathi amma.

At that moment Pichiah and Kavita who had found some space in one of the bullock carts heard distinctly the voice of the zamindar Shankar Dev Rao coming from somewhere in the darkness imploring his son ie Vikram not to leave him and telling him "do not be afraid, I am here with you".Vikram replied "nana, is that you, where are you?", then Shankar Dev Rao's voice and Bukka's voice could be heard "Vikram we are so close to you, do you not feel us?" Vikram while mounting his horse said "I am going to cut down these accursed vines and burn them to the ground, I will rid this house of the scourge that has plagued us", then Rudra's voice was heard saying "please... please... do not kill us,... (sound of weeping)... we are not dead, we have taken a different form". Vikram asked in desperation "which form have you taken?" The reply that everyone of those fleeing the accursed house heard was "we are now alive in the very vines you want to destroy". Vikram stared into the darkness with tears rolling down his cheeks. He heard his father once again

"Vikram you will always be fond of me, I represent to you all the sins you never had the courage to commit, what do you know about virtue because in order to know virtue you must acquaint yourself with vice, I have no repentance because I have all the power to sin eternally". All that Vikram managed to utter was "Oh God...Oh God...Oh God..". Finally he and those around him knew that their house ie the zamindar's mansion, had turned into a living graveyard with their near and dear ones permanently incarcerated in the vampire vine that caused their death, that vine which grew out of the small egg shaped blood ruby like seeds which some of them had planted on a full moon night.

As the bullockcarts and those who were on horse back started to leave, a hideous, malevolent kind of laughter rang through the air. Vikram Dev Rao sat on a horse and after ensuring all the bullockcarts were on the move, he turned his horse towards the outhouse in which Malli was kept, he reached the outhouse and broke the door down. Malli was sitting on her bed, on seeing Vikram, she said "take the diamonds and the single large, hen's egg sized blood ruby like seed, place this seed in an iron chest and cover it with kumkum ie vermillion, then bury the iron chest in a room deep under the ground, do not try to discard the blood ruby seed, because if you do that it will find you". Vikram said "I cannot ask for your forgiveness for what my father did to you, but you are free to go where -ever you please as of this moment". Malli said "I have nowhere to go, you have to take me with you and treat me as a member of your family", that is the prayaschittam (atonement for what was done to me by your father) you have to do.

All of a sudden, a peculiar kind of hot wind had picked up speed and with the wind howling in the background coupled with the hideous laughter, it was as if the gates of hell had opened to let out a few while the remaining were left behind, in a living graveyard ruled by the vampire vine. Raktabeeja and Ugrasena two of the closest bodyguards of the late zamindar, in a fit of sheer hatred and anger went close to a stunted tree from which the vines emerged, the moment their axes touched down on the trunk of the tree, it screamed like a human being in excruciating pain and in a matter of seconds, the vines which appeared inert and motionless came alive and wrapped themselves around both the bodyguards while their suckers sank deeper and deeper into the bodyguards and consumed them in full view of those who watched in horror leaving their dying screams as a diabolical memory etched on the minds of the living.

That night the convoy halted at the residence of the zamindar of Rajanpalli. On arrival in Rajanpalli, Maheshwari Devi on seeing Yamini Devi (who had come directly from the temple of the Godess Sri Sivagami Sundari Amman to her brother's house in Rajanpalli), her daughter Lakshmi Devi, Bramarambha Devi and a host of others, burst into a torrent of tears. Slowly by slowly, she narrated the series of events that overtook them that night to all those who sat around her and who had consoled her. They stared in disbelief at one another, they could not believe what they were hearing, never in their life had they heard something similar to this and yet Maheshwari Devi was too senior a member of the family to be taken lightly and people knew her to be a mature person whose integrity was above question, she was not a rumour monger nor was she a story teller. While she was relating what happened, Vikram Dev Rao lay on a bed, silent, his mind in turmoil.

After lying motionless on the bed for a long time Vikram Dev Rao sent for Malli and as soon as she entered the bedroom he asked her to sit down. Then he asked her "why did all this happen?" She said "your father's men, on his instructions murdered Muthu my lover, then your father kept me in the outhouse and ravished me daily. He could have taken the diamonds and the blood red ruby like seeds and spared Muthu and me, but he did not. He, his son Bukka and his grandson Rudra inflicted terrible pain and humiliation on me. Then one day I had enough of this day to day torture, I cursed the three of them and I decided to teach him, his progeny and those with a similar bent of mind a lesson. I told him that (I had learnt of a tantric vidhi ie an occult method, which could make the small bird's egg shaped blood red ruby like seeds to come alive, when I overheard a conversation between two senior members of the council of elders in the Kingdom of the Sun God) whoever participated in the tantric vidhi ie occult ritual and planted the small, bird's egg shaped blood ruby seeds soaked in the blood of an animal which had been slaughtered for that purpose, would reap wealth beyond their imagination". But in reality, those who participated in the ritual including your father, half brother and your sister-in-law on the say so of her husband and their son including the household staff and those who sowed the seeds were marked people. Thereafter, their gruesome and horrifying death was inevitable and irrevocable". The rest had just one option, to leave that accursed house and never to come back. After a long pause Malli said "the blood ruby egg shaped seeds was the currency we used in the Kingdom of the Sun God, to buy and to sell anything just like cowrie shells were used in ancient times, but noone knew that each seed held a dark secret, that **when a seed is soaked in fresh blood and planted it comes alive and destroys the person who sowed it**. The vampire vine 'reacts' violently, only when its existance is threatened by day when someone tries to cut it down with a machete to clear a passage or hacks at the trunk with an axe to clear the land or for any other purpose. On the other hand at night it 'acts' like a dangerous predator on the hunt, the only difference is that the vampire vine hunts at night even if it is not hungry, especially human beings **just for the sake of devouring them and acquiring their atma or their souls, it then becomes a repository of their souls. If the vampire vine in which a soul or an atma is incarcerated is cut down or destroyed, then that soul will be lost forever, it will cease to exist. However with the passage of several thousands of years the soul of**

a person incarcerated by the vampire vine can hope for salvation ie hopes to be liberated by a divine act of mercy. Under the circumstances if you want the souls or the atma of those who are incarcerated by the vampire vine to gain salvation or to be liberated from the clutches of the vampire vine at some very distant point of time, do not attempt to cut down or destroy the vampire vine.

On the other hand if the seed was sown without the blood ritual, it formed just an impenetrable border, a living carnivorous border like the border that protected the inhabitants of the Kingdom of the Sun God. The Tantric or the occult vidhi or method that made the vampire vine into a repository of souls was based on what the council of elders had learnt many centuries ago from Mayong, the land of black magic and from occult practitioners at the Chausath temple in Hirapur."

Sorcery and black magic: Mayong the secluded, untouched, eerie village in ancient Assam on the banks of the Brahmaputra River was famous for sorcery, the cradle of black magic for centuries. While villagers pass down the skills of farming or craftsmanship to the next generation, the elders in Mayong passed down ancient secrets pertaining to sorcery and black magic to their youth. Mayong originated from the Sanskrit word "maya" which means illusion. In Mayong people had been transformed into animals, monstrous beasts have been tamed and others have disappeared into thin air by uttering the "Luki-Mantra." The Mughal Emperor Muhammad Shah's army of 10,000 soldiers and horsemen perished because of witchcraft in a location close to Mayong where human sacrifice ie "Narabali", nara means head, bali means sacrifice, was used to propitiate Yoginis (Yoginis are a group of forest spirits or mother goddesses of the forest, in the 9th to the 12thcenturies, Yoginis were semi demonic, semi divine goddesses representing various forms of shakti) and spirits. Witch doctors in Mayong treated diseases, injuries, pain with a metal dish and spells. The metal dish was used to suck out the pain from someone's body. The witch doctor was also adept in locating lost objects. The other place from which the council of elders learnt the rituals, mantras and the tantric occult vidhi ie method, was from the practitioners of this vidhi in the Chausath temple in Hirapur, located close to Kalinga (modern day Cuttack) the ancient capital of Orissa.

Vikram Dev Rao sat alone on his bed after he swore Malli to silence and permitted her to leave, until he was joined by Maheshwari Devi, he did not tell his wife anything. There was no need for her to know what happened to the souls of those who the vampire vine consumed, he did not want to burden her with unbearable misery, knowing full well that she and Parvathi Devi were closer than sisters. He did not want to tell Maheshwari that the atma or the souls of her closest friend Parvathi, his father Shankar Dev Rao, his half brother Bukka, Bukka and Parvathi's son Rudra and many others were in the possession of the vampire vine for eternity. **This was a horrifying secret that he and Malli alone knew and it was best for everyone that they took the secret to their grave.**

About a fortnight later Vikram Dev Rao, his wife, his mother, Malli and other members of his household staff left Rajanpalli, after leaving the zamindari of Mahadevpalli, in the care of his daughter's father-in-law ie the zamindar of Rajanpalli, to undertake the long journey to Dholapur. In his possession was a large number of diamonds and small egg shaped blood ruby like seeds originally from the Kingdom of the Sun God taken by his late father from Malli. In addition in his possession was sackfulls of small egg shaped blood ruby like seeds collected by Rudra, his bodyguards and Maya along with a sigle large hen's egg sized blood ruby like seed buried in kumkum or vermillion powder in an iron chest, that alone would ensure that it ie the single large egg shaped blood ruby like seed remained sterile for all times to come.

The descendants of Vikram Dev Rao were the erstwhile zamindars of Dholapur (a few kilometres from Pune) until India gained independence and Dholapur became a part and parcel of the Union of India. It is said that even today somewhere in a subterranean room in the vast and princely Dholapur House lies an ancient, heavily chained and locked, iron chest which is chained to the wall so that it cannot be opened or removed. On this chest is a sign of the swastika and a mantra engraved, which is meant to prevent whatever is inside it from inflicting terrible suffering on the zamindar and his family. The door to this underground room was closed centuries ago by tantrics ie those who dabble in the occult, in the presence of Vikram Dev Rao, with a warning that it must not be opened. No member of the erstwhile zamindar's family has ever since gone anywhere near the entrance to the closed and locked cellar, its one and only occupant ie the iron chest with its diabolical secret has remained unopened and undisturbed over the centuries.

A few months after the departure of Vikram Dev Rao and his family their relative Jaganmohan Dev Rao, the zamindar of Rajanpalli got sculptors to make a massive stone edict with a human palm sculpted on it and with the words **"Thaamba ie stop in large letters, in Marathi and below it the words 'do not enter' in smaller letters" inscribed at the base of the palm in Telugu. He also entrusted the head priest or the head poojari of the Sri Sivagami Sundari Amman temple with the hand written, scrolled document that was given to him by Vikram Dev Rao before his departure.** Lakshmi Devi tearfully bade farewell by placing a garland of flowers on the edict, after all she had very fond memories of the house in which she grew up, her grandfather and the others who perished. She remembered her pedda nana the zamindar Shankar Dev Rao who always treated her as his princess. She remembered her mama ie uncle Bukka who treated her with a lot of affection no matter what kind of reputation he had, to her he was always courteous and affectionate. She remembered Parvathi Devi who both her mother and she, truly loved and last but not the least she remembered the carefree days when as youngsters she played for hours on end with her brother Surya and Rudra.

Vikram Dev Rao died at the ripe old age of 90, his wife Maheshwari preceded him ten years earlier, his son Surya married the daughter of the Raja of Kolhapur. Malli married a very wealthy merchant with all fanfare as a member of the zamindar's family. Prior to his death Vikram Dev Rao quietly sold the small egg shaped blood ruby like seeds to the Dutch, the French and the British East India companies, whose representatives bought them (ie the small blood red egg shaped ruby like seeds) under the impression that they were genuine Blood Red Burma Rubies, for a fabulous sum of money. Only Vikram Dev Rao, his son Surya Dev Rao, Malli and Jaganmohan Dev Rao (the zamindar of Rajanpalli) knew the dark and sinister truth.

Back in Mahadevpalli a detachment of the Nizam's soldiers who were passing through Rayalseema a 100 years later in 1838 wanted to take refuge in the mansion to avoid being caught in a suddern hail storm, the commander of the Nizam's forces sent a small detachment of his men to scout around the vast mansion and to see whether they could take shelter in it. His men on horse back approached the zamindar's mansion and were presently surprised to see a light in the main hall, they thought someone was inhabiting or staying in the mansion. As they approached the open door they heard laughter and saw three men and a woman in costly clothes wearing gold jewellery seated on beautiful chairs conversing with one another, while a host of attendants were standing around to attend to them. When the soldiers stepped foot into the house the lamp lights that lit up the main hall flickered and went out, the people they saw disappeared. What could be seen in the moonlight filtereng through the open windows was a dilapidated hall overrun by a kind of creeper or a vine, coated in dirt with massive cobwebs, there was an element of death and decay in that hall.

That was enough to put the fear of God in the soldiers, they retreated much faster than they approached the doorway, got onto their horses and informed their commander that the mansion was in ruins and unfit for them to stay in. Over the years other people who have mistakenly entered the premises and lived to come out, confirmed what the Nizam's soldiers had seen and many others believe that the four people in the main hall that people claimed to have seen, are none other than the zamindar of Mahadevpalli Shankar Dev Rao, his son Bukka Dev Rao, his daughter-in-law Parvathi Devi and their son Rudra Dev Rao and a host of others, all of whom had died in that house under unnatural circumstances some 280 years ago, sometime between the years 1737 to 1738.

"I'm every nightmare you've ever had.
I am your worst dream come true. I am everything you ever were afraid of".

– Pennywise

Chapter 20

Conclusion

Before I conclude, I would like to state that the happenings in Mahadevpalli may come under the realm of fiction, in the absence of any scientific study or proof. However all that happens in this world is not necessarily fictional because it is not backed up by scientifically proven facts, there are known instances where something was thought of as fiction but turned out to be a fact in later years. For example even today across the vast moorland in The British isles there is a bromeliad, a huge and spiky native of Chile called the *Puya chilensis* which like cacti has spines for protection but which it uses for hunting. The plant using its spines, traps animals like domestic sheep with thick fur and because they are unable to extricate themselves, in the absence of food they starve to death. Once the animal falls to the ground and decomposes at the base of the plant, providing highly rich localised food, the plant absorbs it, the process is gruesome as hell. Horticulturists in England have coaxed one such plant to bloom by feeding it a rich dose of liquid fertilizer keeping in mind the fact that feeding it on its natural diet would have brought out a public hue and cry.

On the other hand there is a plant called the Pisonia which flowers only twice a year and subsequently its seeds also ripen only twice a year. In this case the seeds which are small and easy to brush against are extremely sticky and covered with tiny hooks which intertwine with the barbs on the bird's feather, which is not dangerous but when there are twenty or more such seeds hanging on to each wing it becomes extremely difficult for the bird to extricate itself and fly away. Under the circumstances the birds starve while they are hopelessly entangled in a mass of seeds. The sight of dead birds entangled in a ripening bundle of fruits and hanging from the tree like decomposing baubles is a macabre sight. For most predatory plants living on marginal soils means that the plants have to look to other sources for additional nutrients, but in the case of the Pisonia this argument does not hold, because it lives mostly on rich subtropical soils and additionally fertilized by the sea birds who basically dredge up the riches of the sea and cap them all over the place. In other words the Pisonia kills "for the heck of it", the Roman poet Horace ascribed them with "active malevolence". Some people came up with the suggestion that Pisonia seeds are optimised for dispersion by being carried to faroff places while clinging to the bird's feathers, this explains why Pisonia seeds are sticky, however it does not explain why they are murderously sticky, which makes the bird death-to-stickiness ratio bad news for the birds.

Leaving all these accounts aside, on October 23, 2007 the NewIndPress.com, website, posted a bizarre story that came from the village of Patrame, located about 30 kms from the city of Uppinangady, close to Mangalore in the state of Karnataka. The NewIndPress reported that a tree near the village was seen to bend and lift a cow off the ground. The incident happened in the evening on October 18th. The cow had been grazing in the forest when the tree grabbed it, the cowherd watching all the animals ran for help and returned with Anand Gowda the owner of the cow and a group of villagers who chopped down the tree. The Range Forest Officer Mr. Subramanya Rao confirmed that he had received quite a few complaints about cows coming home in the evening with deep gashes, bloody lesions and their tails missing. The locals called the tree "Pili Mara" or "Tiger Tree". Within a few days, reporters from Daijiworld TV went to Patrame to double check the story. According to them on October 18th a young lady called Pushpalatha was walking through the forest in the late afternoon when she saw saw a tree lifting a cow by its hind quarters, the cow was trying to pull itself away from the tree, but the tree was not letting go. Pushpalatha ran to the village and informed her mother who told her not to touch the tree. The cow was rescued only after Vasanna a local farmer cut it down. The reporters also interviewed Ananda Gowda who was applying medicine to cuts and lesions on his cow which was in great pain. Gowda told the reporters that the trees which attacked the cows were known locally as "Pili Mara" and that they were mentioned in folk songs. Another villager Puttanna also recalled that there was another such tree close to the village which was cut to save the animals. Despite all these incidents no indepth inquiry has been done because some people believe that the trees are possessed by evil spirits and any inquiry will be limited and will not reveal the truth. Superstition or no superstition, the presence of such carnivores cannot be ruled out altogether.

It's important to remember that life on earth is beautiful. It's also important to remember that it's frequently horrible, morbid and totally uncaring, the Pili Mara, the Puya chilensis and the Pisonia fall in the second category as does the carnivore of Mahadevpalli.

"There are horrors beyond life's edge that we do not suspect, and once in a while man's evil prying calls them just within our range".

– H. P. Lovecraft

Epilogue

Somewhere in the year 1996 a cowherd called Puttanna was bringing home his cows late one evening, when he heard a cow making a sound as if it was in great distress. On turning back he saw a cow which had fallen on its side and was making a great effort to get up. Something had obviously pushed it to the ground but whatever it was, had withdrawn into the deep jungle on either side of the road. The cowherd did not think it was prudent to investigate the matter any further because it would have become totally dark in a short while. The cow got up by this time on its own, staggered and with great effort followed the cowherd back to the village. There in dim lantern light the cowherd's wife examined the cow, after her husband told her what had happened and she noticed a number of deep lesions and abrasions on the cow's hide through which blood was oozing. The blood continued to ooze because it took quite some time for it to clot. The very same kind of lesions and abrasions that was seen on Shankar Dev Rao, the terrified and dying zamindar of Mahadevpalli some 280 years ago, who had met his doom in the hands of something far more sinister and evil, while taking a dip in an open pond, after walking late at night, around the vast area surrounding his house, on a beautiful moonlit night.

However the incident in 2007 happened in an area close to a village in the midst of forested land about 100 kms from Mangalore, bringing back the often asked question, where does fiction end and where does science which is non-fiction begin. Was the Kingdom of the Sun fictitious, was the method they evolvded to protect themselves a piece of fiction or is it something that will be revealed in due course of time backed up by scientific evidence. All that I can say is that **"Truth Is Stranger Than Fiction"** and you my dear reader must discern for yourself whether what I have written is a piece of fiction or something which has very deep roots in hitherto undiscovered facts. There are periods in our history which belong to the dark ages and it is best that no one tinkers with the past especially with something that is believed to be a myth because by tinkering with the past you may be involuntarily bringing something alive which is the stuff of a horror movie, something that should have remained suppressed and contained within a firmly closed space.

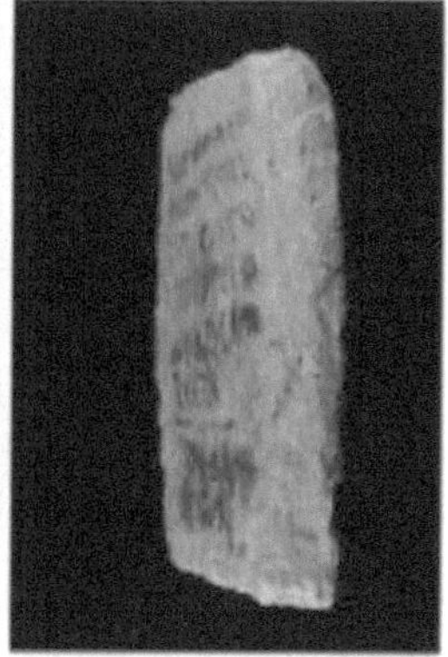

'Do Not Open', Warns Tomb Discovered At UNESCO World Herit...

New Delhi: Can't help but recall the 1999 H...

m.dailyhunt.in

'Do Not Open', Warns Tomb Discovered At UNESCO World Heritage Site In Israel | Is A Curse On Way Towards Us?

The Essence of Horror

Horror is not something we create, nor is it something that jumps out of a closet in a dark room at an ungodly hour. Horror is not something which always advertises its presence with things falling down, windows banging shut or lights going off. It is something far more subtle, more real, more sinister like your shadow, imagine if it were to grow in length every day even if you stood at the same spot, at the same time of the day and when the lighting is similar.

The shadow that grows like a cloak on your back on a day by day basis proportionate to the debauchery and evil you engage in, until it grows to such an extent that it engulfs you, sunlight is blotted out of your life and you are condemned to live in eternal darkness, is the essence of horror. Something that enters your life as a small vice, stays on as a companion, then grows as a master in whose clutches you are until it obliterates "you". Horror is that which will sink deep roots into your subconscious and change you from within to such an extent that you will appear alien to yourself.

END

www.ingramcontent.com/pod-product-compliance
Lightning Source LLC
LaVergne TN
LVHW041019150826
845672LV00001B/134

* 9 7 9 8 8 8 7 4 9 3 1 0 7 *